HAJI of the ELEPHANTS

Haji had risked his life to recapture the mighty Majda Koom from a herd of wild elephants he was leading. In reward, Haji's skill as a handler of elephants had been recognized and he had been made an oozie, as the brown-skinned elephant riders of Burma were called. Not only had he been made an oozie, Haji's greatest wish had been realized when he was given Majda Koom to ride. Majda Koom was the lord of all elephants, and his fame had spread to the far corners of Burma, and even beyond the borders into India and Nepal and China.

But Haji's happiness is shortlived when a new Inspector of the Rangoon Lumber Company arrives and declares Haji is too young to be an oozie. A period of test and trial starts for Haji, which sees him caught up in the terror of the jungle, a charge of wild elephants, and an even more terrifying threat, when he is trapped in a plot set by humans who want to abduct Majda Koom.

HAJI of the ELEPHANTS

by WILLIS LINDQUIST
illustrated by DON MILLER

McGraw-Hill Book Company
New York   St. Louis   San Francisco
Auckland   Düsseldorf
Johannesburg   Kuala Lumpur   London
Mexico   Montreal   New Delhi
Panama   Paris   São Paulo
Singapore   Sydney
Tokyo   Toronto

Library of Congress Cataloging in Publication Date

Lindquist, Willis.
    Haji of the elephants.

    SUMMARY: Haji's greatest wish is realized when he is given a mighty
elephant to ride, but then he enters a terrifying period where he is threatened
by both animals and humans.
    [1. India—Fiction. 2. Elephants—Fiction]
I. Miller, Don,—   II. Title.
PZ7.L6594Haj   [Fic]   76–4804
ISBN 0–07–037892–4 lib. bdg.

This book is a presentation of
The Popcorn Bag
Weekly Reader Book Club

Weekly Reader Book Division offers book clubs for
children from preschool to young adulthood. All
quality hardcover books are selected by a distinguished
Weekly Reader Selection Board.

For further information write to:
Weekly Reader Book Division
1250 Fairwood Avenue
Columbus, Ohio 43216

Weekly Reader Children's Book Club Edition

Publisher's edition: $5.72

Contents

To my little friend
Luis Colon

HAJI of the ELEPHANTS

1

Inspection of the Elephants

The noonday sun blazed down on the elephant camp and the surrounding hills of the jungle. In a large clearing at the edge of the River Yu, thirty-seven elephants and their riders were lined up for inspection. There was no wind, not a cloud in the sky. Not a leaf stirred.

The boy Haji took a deep breath. Large beads of sweat rolled down his brown cheeks as he sat patiently on the head of his elephant, the mighty Majda Koom. For an hour he had waited there in the broiling sun for his turn to move up and have his elephant looked over by the visiting inspector from the Rangoon Lumber Company.

Haji was far too happy to be greatly bothered by the heat. Happiness was like a song within him, for now at

1

last his greatest wish had been realized. Thakin Jensen, the stern white master of the elephant camp, had finally recognized his skill as a handler of elephants and had made him an oozie, as the brown-skinned elephant riders of Burma were called.

Not only had he been made an oozie, but the thakin had also given him the mighty Majda Koom to ride, the lord of all elephants, whose fame had spread to the far corners of Burma—from the Shan Hills in the east to the jade-green forests of Naga in the north, and even beyond the borders into India and Nepal and China.

"Why does it take so long?" complained Haji's friend, Ket Kay, who was squatting on the ground not far away. "The sun is burning me."

Haji looked down at him. Ket Kay, only twelve, seemed so small, so frail, so helpless as he hunkered there in the sun. He wore a turban of faded blue and a loincloth of the same color. He had the largest eyes Haji had ever seen, eyes that were soft and brown, and he had the habit of blinking them so slowly and solemnly that he always looked as though he had much to think about.

"Come into the shade of my elephant," said Haji. "His shadow is small now, but if you sit there next to his front leg . . ."

"Wah!" exclaimed Ket Kay. "I would rather stay here in the sun and cook than be stepped on by an elephant."

Haji laughed. For a moment he had forgotten that Ket Kay was not one of the elephant people, but a visitor from the Valley of Ten Villages where the rice farmers lived. They knew nothing of elephants.

"He will not step on you," said Haji. "If you lean against his leg he will know you are there. Then he will be very careful not to move."

As Ket Kay edged a little closer his big eyes grew wide with fear. "Are you sure it is safe, Haji? I do not like to be so close to something so big."

At that moment Majda Koom swung his trunk out toward Ket Kay. The boy jumped back just in time.

"Majda Koom knows you are my friend, Ket Kay. He is reaching out to touch you and get your smell. It is his way of saying hello. Hold out your hand now so he can smell it."

Ket Kay hesitated. "But this is the big bull that was leading a wild herd of elephants only a few days ago. And is it not true that he killed the oozies sent out to catch him?"

"No one was there to see how they were killed," answered Haji. "When Majda Koom was with the wild elephants he was wild. But now he is with tame elephants again and he is tame. Hold out your hand so he can make friends with you."

Timidly Ket Kay did as he was told. The great elephant slowly reached out with his trunk, touched the boy's hand gently and got his smell.

"Good," said Haji. "Now sit down by his leg and have no fear. He is as gentle now as he was years ago when I learned to walk by holding onto his trunk."

At last convinced, Ket Kay stepped into the elephant's shadow and sat down, leaning against one of the front legs. A few minutes later he said, "Ayee, Haji, it is

3

much cooler here in the shade. Come down and sit with me."

"It would be good to be in the shade, but I am not sure it would be all right. All the other oozies are still on their elephants and . . . and. . . ."

All at once Majda Koom reached up, encircled Haji's waist with his trunk, and lowered him gently into the shade between his front legs.

Ket Kay watched in amazement. "Did you tell him to put you down here?"

Haji smiled. "That was Majda Koom's idea. He understands more talk than you think, and sometimes he still likes to take care of me as he did when I was small."

Ket Kay leaned forward to see Haji on the other side of the elephant's leg. "The oozies are right. They say that Majda Koom loves you above all others. Does it not make you feel proud?"

"It makes my love for him even stronger. Is he not the mightiest of all elephants?"

Ket Kay nodded. "I never knew before that an elephant could be so big. Back home in my village I have heard of him all my life. There is a saying among the villagers that Majda Koom stands over all other elephants as a mountain stands over the hills. I have heard them say his big tusks are as thick around as the pillars in the pagoda temple at Chinwa. This I never believed. But now I have seen and I know it is true—all that they have said."

The giant tusker towering over them suddenly made

a soft rumbling sound that came from deep within him, and began swinging his trunk from side to side in front of them.

"Why is he doing that?" asked Ket Kay.

Haji pointed to the elephant next in line, who was just moving forward to be inspected. "Majda Koom has been in many inspections before and he knows our turn is next. He is glad it will soon be over so he can get out of the hot sun."

"He is glad? How do you know that?"

"When an elephant makes the soft rumbling sound it means he is pleased."

Ket Kay shook his head almost sadly. "I wish I had been born in an elephant camp like you were, Haji. You know so much about elephants."

"All I know I have learned from my father. He was Majda Koom's oozie for thirty years, and he would still be his oozie had a tree not fallen on him."

The accident had happened over two years ago, and since then Haji's father had been a helpless cripple, living with Haji's mother and his small sister in Chinwa, in the Valley of Ten Villages.

Minutes passed. As Haji watched the inspection he became more and more restless.

"Something is wrong?" asked Ket Kay.

"The new inspector is taking too long, and he has no feeling for elephants."

Ket Kay blinked his big eyes in surprise. "Why do you say that?"

5

"No one who cares about elephants would want them to stand in the sun for so long. Always before, the elephants have been lined up in the shade on inspection days. Thakin Jensen has always seen to that. But today the inspector gives the orders."

The inspector was a man of great importance, for he came directly from the home office of the Rangoon Lumber Company, the company which operated all the jungle camps and owned all the elephants. Like Thakin Jensen, the inspector was an Englishman. Both wore sun helmets and white shirts and khaki shorts. But they did not look alike. The inspector was fat, and as the two stood side by side at the place of inspection, Thakin Jensen was a whole head taller than the visitor.

Haji watched until the elephant being inspected had moved to one side, and the thakin gave him the signal to bring up Majda Koom.

"Move, Ket Kay," Haji warned as he sprang to his feet and began his advance.

The elephant followed. Majda Koom reached out and took hold of Haji's hand with the tip of his trunk, as he had done so many times before during the years of Haji's childhood. For Haji it was like holding hands with a big brother, and it gave him a good warm feeling inside as they walked along together. Haji felt like smiling his happy smile, but the stern look on the inspector's round, red face warned him against it.

That didn't matter, Haji told himself, although he did feel a bit uneasy. The important thing, after all, was

6

the inspection, and he knew he had good reason to be proud of his elephant's condition.

At sunup that morning he had taken Majda Koom to the river and bathed him from trunk to tail. He had examined his ears inside and out for blood-sucking ticks. He had searched for thorns and bamboo splinters in the giant pads of the elephant's feet, and had polished the nails of his toes till they shone like glass. Last of all, with fine sand from the river, he had rubbed the great tusks until they became gleaming shafts of creamy white ivory. Majda Koom had never looked better.

No fault could be found with his elephant, Haji felt sure. Yet, it was plain to be seen, from the sour expression on the inspector's red face, that he was not at all pleased. What troubled Haji even more was the fact that the man was staring, not at the elephant, but at him.

Haji suddenly felt tense. He came to a halt before the two men. At the same moment the elephant's trunk slipped around his waist. Majda Koom lifted him high and held him there before the inspector for several moments before lowering him to his head.

Laughter came from a group of oozies squatting nearby in the shade. Haji would have joined in their laughter, had he dared, for it was plain to all that Majda Koom had taken this way to show his love and his pride in his new oozie. Even Thakin Jensen, for a moment, wore a tight little smile.

The inspector's red face became even redder. He was

7

so annoyed he almost choked. "Who is being inspected here, the boy or the elephant?" he demanded.

Thakin Jensen ignored the question. "This is the famous Majda Koom, Inspector," he said proudly. "Had you not been new in Burma you would most certainly have recognized him at once. In all my years in Burma I have never had the pleasure of knowing a more remarkable animal."

"Yes, yes. A truly magnificent beast, I am sure," agreed the inspector, as Majda Koom slowly turned around so that he could be seen from all sides. "But where is his oozie?"

At that moment the brown-skinned chief of the oozies, Oo Yan, came up and handed the thakin Majda Koom's record book. Every working elephant had its own record book. The thakin flipped the book open. "This bull was born here in camp thirty-eight years ago," he said. "Health—perfect. If you were to study his work record over the years, you would find that he has moved more logs than any other two elephants put together. His height at the shoulders—"

"Never mind all that!" snapped the inspector. "I should like, if you please, to have an answer to my question. What about the elephant's oozie? Where is he?"

"Majda Koom's oozie? You are looking at him, Inspector." Thakin Jensen pointed to Haji.

"What's that you say? Am I to understand that a child of ten or eleven—"

"Thirteen, Inspector; almost fourteen now, although it is true he is small for his age."

The inspector gasped. He had to open and close his mouth several times before he could find his voice, his eyes popping, his face even redder than before. "Are you saying," he roared, "that—that this child—"

"Were it not for this child, Inspector, Majda Koom would not be here for you to inspect today," said Thakin Jensen slowly and very politely. "He would still be off in the jungle somewhere, leading a herd of wild elephants."

"I—I don't understand," stammered the inspector. "Leading a herd of wild elephants, did you say?"

Haji let out his breath. He felt better, knowing Thakin Jensen was ready to defend his right to be an oozie.

"The details are all here in this book, Inspector," said the thakin. "For thirty years the father of this boy was the oozie of Majda Koom, then was crippled for life by a falling tree. I sent him and his family away, to live in the village of Chinwa in the valley. Shortly after that the elephant began acting strangely. Some said he was going mad."

"Mad?" asked the inspector. "He became dangerous?"

"Not exactly dangerous. He came into camp night after night. Oo Yan here, my chief oozie, believes Majda Koom came into camp searching for the only two people in the world he ever loved—his oozie and the son, this boy Haji." Thakin Jensen turned to the chief of the oozies who stood by his side. "Is that not what you told me, Oo Yan?"

"It is even as you said, Thakin," replied Oo Yan.

"Such was Majda Koom's grief when he could not find them that he ran off into the jungle and became wild."

Thakin Jensen turned again to the inspector. "It wasn't long after that that he joined a herd of wild elephants."

"You sent men out to recapture him, of course?"

Thakin Jensen nodded. "I did. Three of my best oozies went out, one at a time. The first searched through the jungle for months without finding him. The last two never came back. So far as we know, they are both dead. Whether they were killed by Majda Koom or by other wild elephants of the herd no one will ever know."

The fat inspector mopped his red face with a handkerchief and looked at the elephant with new interest. "If your reputation with the company were not the best, Jensen, I would find it difficult to believe. Just how long did the elephant run with the wild herd?"

"Over two years," answered the thakin. "We heard nothing about him in all that time. Then, quite recently, word came that Majda Koom had been seen and was leading a herd of wild elephants down the valley, raiding the rice fields of the villages. It was then that this boy Haji did what our best oozies had not been able to do. He recaptured Majda Koom and brought him back here. That was less than two weeks ago."

The inspector shook his head. "Only two weeks ago! Yet this animal is as tame and gentle as any of the others. How can that be?"

"That is a miracle for which there can be only one explanation—his great love for this boy Haji," declared the thakin. "It does not surprise me for I can remember when Haji, as a small child, used to climb on the elephant's tusks and use his trunk as a swing. I've seen the two go off into the jungle together to play, and I've seen them swim together in the river."

The inspector cleared his throat. "Well, that is all very interesting to be sure, but—"

"In my report you will see how this boy risked his life to recapture the elephant," Thakin Jensen went on. "The company owes Haji a great deal."

The inspector was becoming annoyed again. His face had darkened to a purplish red. "That may be," he said. "And I must say, Jensen, that you did a very understandable thing in making the boy a—a temporary oozie as a kind of reward, shall we say. But now we must be practical. Now we must consider what is best for the company. You will surely agree with that, Jensen."

"Of course," agreed the thakin.

"Then it should be clear to you, as it is to me, that now we must go about the business of finding an experienced oozie as soon as possible, one wise enough to get the most out of this remarkable beast."

Haji forgot to breathe. What was the inspector saying? That he was only to be oozie for a few days? That soon Majda Koom would be taken from him and given to another oozie? It couldn't be! It couldn't!

"No, Thakin!" cried Haji aloud, forgetting his manners. "You told me—"

Thakin Jensen shot him an angry glance. "That will do, Haji," he said firmly. "The inspection is over. You may go."

2

A Test for Haji

Haji stared at the man, stunned. Was Thakin Jensen now turning against him, too? The question was so frightening that Haji suddenly felt sick. He was only dimly aware of the fact that his elephant had turned and was carrying him off into the cool shade at the edge of the jungle.

There the oozies were gathered. They looked at him, waiting for him to speak. He turned his head away. The thought of losing Majda Koom filled him with cold fear.

As the great elephant lowered him gently to the ground, a wrinkled oozie, the oldest in camp, came up to him.

"Do not let the red-faced one trouble you," he said gently. "He does not understand. He is new. He knows nothing."

"Ayee, that is true," said another, as the oozies gathered around Haji. "He knows nothing, and he makes trouble because he does not know that he knows nothing."

"It is even so," agreed the wrinkled one. "You must have patience and trust in the thakin."

Haji felt a little better, knowing that the oozies were on his side. He swallowed hard. "But—but the thakin has been ordered to—to find a new oozie for Majda Koom."

A thin smile played on the lips of the wrinkled one. "It is in my mind that Majda Koom may have some say in this," he said. "Never in all my years have I known another elephant like him. When he is not pleased he can be stubborn. He wants but one master, and the master he has chosen is you, little brother."

Another oozie said, "It may be that Majda Koom would go wild again if Haji were taken from him. The thakin will have to explain this to the red-faced one."

Haji shook his head sadly. "The red-faced one will not listen."

"How can you know that? Do not forget the thakin has great wisdom. He has ways to convince. Look!" The old one pointed to the two Englishmen in the field.

They were walking away together. It was plain that the thakin had much to say, and the red-faced inspector seemed to be listening. Haji watched anxiously until they disappeared among the tall palms by the river.

Drawing a deep breath, he turned to take his elephant to a tree and chain him there, for Thakin Jensen had given him strict orders never to leave Majda Koom loose so long as the wild elephant herd was in the vicinity.

At that moment Ket Kay ran up, offering him a green coconut, slashed open at one end for drinking. Haji took a long drink of the cool coconut milk. How good it tasted in his hot, dry mouth!

He turned to pour some of it into the end of Majda Koom's trunk so that he could have a taste of it, too. But his elephant had wandered off and joined one of the small groups of elephants standing nearby in the shade.

None of their oozies were with them. Not that they needed to be, for elephants were creatures of the night, and during the heat of the day it was natural for them to stand quietly in the shade and rest.

Haji hurried to his elephant and led him to a large fig tree and chained him there by one of his hind legs. "I am sorry, big brother," he said. "When the wild elephants have gone so far away they can no longer call to you in the night, then the thakin says you are to go free."

"Can Majda Koom really understand what you say?" asked Ket Kay.

"Elephants always like to hear the voice of their oozies. The oozies have a saying that elephants listen better than their wives do, and they never talk back."

"They do have big ears," said Ket Kay, laughing. He looked back to where the oozies were standing. "Haji, why are the oozies waiting?"

"Waiting? They are not waiting."

"Then why don't they take their elephants into the jungle as they do on other days and drag the logs?"

Haji shook his head. Elephants were used to drag the heavy logs of teakwood to the river where they could be floated downstream to the sawmill. But the logs lay widely scattered and some distance away. To reach them would take time, an hour or more, and the inspector had already taken more than half a day.

"It is too late to start working now," explained Haji.

"Then there is nothing more to do," cried Ket Kay. "Now we can cool off in the river and—"

"No," said Haji. It would have been great fun to swim in the river and rest on the cool bank. But there was no time for that, and Haji was not in the mood for fun. The fear of losing Majda Koom was like an angry bee buzzing around in his head. It would not leave him alone.

Ket Kay, puzzled, looked at him closely. "You are not feeling well?"

Haji tried to smile. "There is work to do. A good oozie must always think first of his elephant. Majda Koom will be hungry again in a few hours, and we must have food ready for him then. Come."

Ket Kay followed in silence as Haji led the way into the jungle. With long sharp *dahs,* as their jungle knives were called, they cut the sweet growing branches of trees and the tender green tops of young bamboo. They carried load after load back to camp, piling it under the giant fig tree where Majda Koom had been chained for the night.

15

When at last they had finished, they were sweaty and tired and out of breath. They took a swift dip in the river to cool off and get rid of the hot sticky feeling.

By that time the sun was already lowering in the west, turning the river into liquid gold. A light breeze had sprung up. Overhead, large white egrets were flying, their necks gracefully curved and their long legs trailing. These storklike birds had spent the day hunting frogs and fish and small wiggly things among the reeds in the wading pools and marshes and were now streaking across the sky to their evening roosting places high in the palms by the river.

Many of the oozies had already hobbled their elephants, chaining their front legs loosely together to keep them from wandering too far away, and had sent them off into the jungle to forage for themselves during the night.

Hurrying back to Majda Koom, Haji took him to the river for a drink, and then led him back to the fig tree again. He was about to chain the elephant to the tree once again when he heard voices.

"Oo Yan comes, and some of the oozies with him," said Ket Kay. "What can he want of you?"

Haji felt a sudden chill. He had no fear of Oo Yan himself, for the man had been his father's closest friend and was almost like a member of his own family. But Oo Yan was also chief of the oozies, and he would not be coming now unless it was on a business of some importance.

As usual, Oo Yan was splendidly dressed, his turban of white silk, and his white coat of authority neatly

16

starched with rice water and spotlessly clean. He came in swift strides, his face clouded with anger.

He raised his hand. "Do not chain him!" he said sternly. "He is not to be chained tonight."

Haji stared in amazement. "But—but, Maung Oo Yan, only yesterday you warned me to keep Majda Koom tied by day as well as by night so long as the herd of wild elephants is near. Have the wild ones gone away?"

"They are still near," declared the wrinkled oozie. "Last night we heard them in the hills just beyond the river."

"True," said another. "Majda Koom would have joined them had he been able. We saw how he fought to break free from the chain that held him."

"What the elephant would do or what he would not do can only be monkey's chatter now," said Oo Yan. "It means nothing. It can change nothing. I have been given an order. I have given that order to Haji, and now it is for him to obey."

Haji nodded. He knew Oo Yan did not like the order any more than he did. "It shall be as you say," he said in a voice hardly louder than a whisper.

"And should Majda Koom run off with the herd of wild elephants, what then would the red-faced one expect of us?" asked the wrinkled one.

"That is for him to say," answered Oo Yan. "What is to be . . . will be." To make it plain there was no more to be said on the subject, he turned and walked swiftly away.

The oozies followed, but more slowly. They drifted

17

away in twos and threes, grumbling among themselves about the red-faced inspector. Most of them headed for the cooking fires where their evening meals of fish and boiled rice were being prepared for them.

Haji and Ket Kay exchanged glances.

Ket Kay looked frightened. "What can you do now, Haji?" he asked. "What if Majda Koom does run away?"

Haji was too mixed up to answer questions. All he knew for certain was that he had no choice but to obey the command Oo Yan had passed on to him. Kneeling, he unfastened the chain from the trunk of the fig tree and used it to chain the front legs of his elephant loosely together.

Majda Koom knew from long experience that the chain on his front legs meant freedom. To show his pleasure, he made small whistling and chirping sounds through his trunk—the sounds of a happy elephant. Yet he was not in a hurry to go. He seemed perfectly content to remain and feed on the fodder piled before him.

The sun was setting, and Ket Kay became restless. "It's time for us to eat, too," he said. "Are you coming?"

Haji shook his head.

"Should I bring you some rice?"

Again Haji shook his head. Food did not interest him. All that mattered at the moment was to be near his elephant, to be able to reach out and touch him and talk to him and keep him company.

Darkness came quickly. Fireflies began twinkling their greenish lights on every side of him, and from a distance came the faint clickity-click, tok, tok, tok of elephant *kalouks,* or wooden bells.

Each of the working elephants had a kalouk hanging from his neck, and each kalouk had a different sound, for every oozie made his own elephant's bell. Majda Koom's had been made years ago by Haji's father, hollowed out of a flat chunk of teakwood with two clappers, one hanging on each side.

The stars came out. An evening breeze off the river brought a damp chill and the smells of reeds and marshes. Haji slapped at a mosquito on his arm. There were so many mosquitoes buzzing around him that he was tempted to light a fire to drive them off. But he didn't. Majda Koom did not enjoy fires and smoke.

"Why were you given your freedom so suddenly tonight?" Haji asked his elephant.

Majda Koom kept right on eating. His only response was the soft rumbling sound of an elephant well pleased with his dinner.

"That red-faced one, he had something to do with this. He said I was too young to be oozie. He would make trouble for—"

The sound of footsteps came from behind. Then he heard Byoo's cheerful voice. "Who are you talking to?"

"To Majda Koom."

Byoo, his childhood playmate and closest friend in the elephant camp, was a bit older than Haji and almost a whole head taller. Haji could not see his friend's face in the darkness, a face as round and as merry as the moon's, but he could almost feel the warmth of Byoo's big smile.

"Where is your little friend from the village?" asked Byoo.

"Ket Kay? The jungle still frightens him a little at night. He stays close to the oozies and their campfires when darkness comes."

"It may be that the mosquitoes bother him," said Byoo cheerfully as he slapped at one. "Come to our campfire. The boys are waiting for you."

Haji looked at the elephant, who was no more than a shapeless mass in the darkness. "I was going to stay here with Majda Koom and—"

"When an elephant is hungry he listens more to his stomach than he does to his heart," answered Byoo. "Majda Koom needs no company while he is eating."

"But—but why is he being freed tonight? What is the meaning of it?"

"This much I know," replied Byoo, suddenly becoming serious and lowering his voice. "The thakin and the red-faced one have had angry words. The boy who helps the cook in the thakin's house has big ears. He may have something to say of all this when he comes to our fire."

Haji leaped to his feet. It would be better to learn the truth from the cook's helper at the boys' campfire than to stay where he was and be troubled by questions he could not answer.

He gave Majda Koom an affectionate pat on the trunk and followed Byoo into the darkness. They moved swiftly for a time along a well-worn jungle path, their bare feet hardly making a sound.

Somewhere in the lonely hills far away a jackal howled at the rising moon. A wild pig squealed. Then came its death screams, then silence again. A tiger had made its kill.

Haji paid little attention to the kill, for he saw flickering firelight on the leaves up ahead, and he was anxious to hear what the cook's helper had to say.

As he and Byoo entered the clearing a hail of friendly greetings came from the boys squatting about the fire.

"What kept you so long, Haji?" asked one.

Haji smiled weakly, trying to hide the uneasiness churning within him. Even here, where he could speak freely with boys his own age, there was little he cared to say.

Most of the boys were *paijaiks,* as the ground helpers were called. They handled the heavy drag chains, fastening them to the teak logs that were to be dragged to the river. They took their orders from the oozies who rode the elephants.

They, too, loved elephants. They looked forward to the day when they, also, would be made oozies and have elephants to ride. So it was natural that they should look up to Haji with great respect.

"Have you nothing to say, Haji?" asked one of his friends.

Haji licked his dry lips. "All I know is that the red-faced one does not like me."

"Is he trying to make trouble for you?" asked another one.

It was a question no one could answer until the cook's helper joined them a few minutes later. He came running and out of breath.

"Never have I known Thakin Jensen to be so angry," he said, taking his place by the fire.

Haji leaned toward him. "Why did the red-faced one order Majda Koom to be set free?" he asked.

"He did not order it," replied the boy. "The order was given by Thakin Jensen."

For a moment there was a stunned silence. Haji was so completely mixed up he hardly knew what to think.

"Thakin Jensen gave the order?" he asked. "But why?"

"To prove you are a good oozie. He said Majda Koom's love for you is so strong he would never run away with the wild ones now that he has found you again."

"What did the red-faced one say to that?" asked Byoo.

"He laughed. He said only a fool would believe such a tale. He said there was only one way the thakin could prove that he spoke the truth . . . and that was to free the elephant now. If Haji could go out in the morning and bring Majda Koom back, then he would earn the right to be oozie. But should the elephant run off with the wild ones, the red-faced one warned, then the thakin would have to pay for the loss of the elephant out of his own wages. It was then the thakin called in Oo Yan and ordered him to free Majda Koom at once."

"Wah!" said one of the boys, and they all looked anxiously at Haji. "The red-faced one means to test you," said one.

Suddenly, before Haji could answer, they all heard the deep mellow tones of Majda Koom's kalouk. For several minutes they listened as the clickity-click, tok, tok, tok of the elephant's wooden bell faded into the distance. Haji knew what that meant. Majda Koom had finished his dinner and was now moving off into the jungle.

One of the boys turned to Haji. "What will Majda Koom do tonight when he is out there and he hears the wild ones calling?"

Haji leaned forward and stirred the fire thoughtfully with a long stick, sending up a swirl of sparks. "He might answer their call and go to them," he said. "Majda Koom was their leader for many months and he must have many friends among them."

"Are you afraid he might run away with them?"

Byoo laughed. "Why should he be afraid? Have you not seen how Majda Koom watches over him? Was there ever an elephant with greater love for his oozie?"

Haji smiled. It was good that the thakin and Byoo had so much faith in Majda Koom's love for him. Yet he could not forget that Majda Koom had been running free in the jungle with the wild herd for many months, and he probably loved his free life with the wild ones.

3

A Mysterious Campfire

Haji could not sleep. Long after the campfires had burned down to glowing embers he lay twisting and turning restlessly on the mat flooring in the hut of the wrinkled one. The night breezes finally died. A hushed stillness fell over the jungle camp. The only sound he could hear was the steady deep breathing of the old one and his wife on the other side of the room.

All at once came another sound that sent a chill through him and he sat up with a jerk. He listened, holding his breath. Faintly, in the distance, the sound came again—the trumpeting of the wild-elephant herd.

Ket Kay threw off his blanket and sat up, too. "What is it?" he whispered.

24

"Wild elephants,". said Haji. "Calling for Majda Koom."

"Will he go to them?"

"He might."

"What will you do?"

"What all good oozies are expected to do. When morning comes I will go out in search of my elephant." Trying to discourage his friend from asking more questions, Haji lay back and, covering himself with his blanket, pretended to fall asleep.

Haji was up with the first hint of gray in the eastern sky. The morning air had a cool, washed freshness, and the gray world of the jungle was filled with the gurgling of water over rocks in a nearby brook.

"Wait, Haji!" whispered Ket Kay as he came down the bamboo ladder.

Haji waited, not at all pleased. He had far to go, and he could move faster alone. "The jungle is strange to you, Ket Kay. I go swiftly and I do not follow an easy trail."

Ket Kay stood silent for a moment. "Have you forgotten your promise, Haji?"

In the dim light Haji could see the disappointment on his friend's face. He felt sorry for him. "Please understand me, Ket Kay. If harm should come to you, the blame will be on my head. I have no way of protecting you. I carry no weapons. I have nothing but swift feet to save me."

"Last night at their fires the oozies said that if Majda

Koom had joined with the wild herd, this would be a morning to remember. That is why I would hold you to your promise."

Haji took a deep breath. "A promise is a promise. But if you must come, you will do as I say. If I raise my hand so, it means silence, not a word whispered, not a cough or a sneeze, not even another step taken."

Ket Kay nodded. "I hear you."

Before following the trail of his elephant, Haji brought a handful of rice and a half coconut shell of fresh water to the little white shrine at the edge of the river. It was his offering to the nats, the evil jungle spirits, to win their favor, for their mischief-making and their power to do harm was well known.

Majda Koom's trail led up into the high ridges that stood against the sky like dark jagged walls. These ridgetops had long been one of his favorite feeding grounds for tender green leaves and branches. Here and there he had stripped great slabs of juicy bark from young trees.

In the half-light, just before sunrise, they moved swiftly and silently, following the elephant's tracks along a rocky ledge and down into a narrow valley deep with shadows, and across an angry stream of plunging white water. They had to cross it by leaping from one slippery rock to another through mists of blinding icy spray. By the time they reached the grassy bank on the other side, they were soaked through and shivering with cold.

Just as Haji started out again at a swift trot, Ket Kay

called to him. "Why do we have to go so fast, Haji?" he asked.

Haji pointed to the ground. "Look! Majda Koom's tracks are deep and far apart. He was going fast here. His trail may be long. That is why we must hurry."

The trail of Majda Koom led them through a thicket of thorny brush. The thorns tore at their loincloths and jabbed and stabbed and scratched their bare legs until Ket Kay cried out in pain. But they did not stop.

They began climbing again, over rolling green hills, which rose higher and higher—mostly open grassland dotted with a few giant teak trees and pines. Running through the tall grass, they were suddenly startled by the flapping and squawking of a peacock frightened from her nest of eggs. She flew off screaming in protest.

"Sorry, little sister," cried Haji. "No harm was meant to you."

There were five beautiful tan-colored eggs, with reddish brown speckles, in a nest of dry grass and feathers. Ket Kay stopped to admire them.

"No, Ket Kay," cried Haji. "Come away, or the eggs will cool before the hen comes back to them."

To Haji, the small living things in their shells were a part of the jungle he loved, for the jungle was more than a home to him. It was a place of freedom and joy, of danger as well as adventure, and he loved all creatures, great and small, who shared it with him.

Still climbing, they came at last to great slopes of bamboo. It was another of Majda Koom's favorite eating places, for he liked nothing better than the feathery leaves and branches of young bamboo. Here on this slope he usually ate his fill and then took a nap.

Haji was secretly well pleased that the elephant had not crossed the River Yu and gone west with the herd of wild elephants. Instead, he had gone east, going farther and farther away from the herd, following his normal pattern of eating at his favorite places. Now, if he had also taken a nap right here on the slopes of bamboo, that would be even further proof that the wild elephants were no longer of great importance to him.

Searching the ground carefully, Haji finally found a place at the edge of a clump of bamboo where a large patch of grass had been flattened. He smiled and pointed it out to Ket Kay.

"This is his bed," he explained cheerfully. "Here is where he slept last night."

Ket Kay blinked slowly and thoughtfully. "I did not know elephants lie down to sleep."

"They like to sleep on the ground for a little every night."

Ket Kay looked up at Haji with greater admiration than ever. "I wish I knew as much about elephants as you do," he said wistfully.

"Listen!" said Haji, raising his hand for silence.

Faintly, they could hear the hollow clicking and clacking of wooden elephant bells. After listening intently for several moments, Haji shook his head. "Majda Koom's kalouk has a different sound. It may be that we can hear it from the top of the hill. Come!"

Ket Kay followed him up a steep slope and out on a shelf of umber rock at the very top of the hill, the highest point in the jungle for miles around.

Haji remembered hearing his father and the wrinkled one and Oo Yan talking about how fine it would be to build a pagoda temple here on this very shelf rock. The statue of the Holy One could then look down on the world of the jungle below—the world of green hills and valleys, stretching out in every direction as far as the eye could see. The hushed stillness that brooded over the high place gave Haji a feeling of peace and of being far removed from the world below.

The gentle tolling of elephant kalouks, dozens of them, came from all sides, all blending in together— sounding rather like the distant musical babbling of a mountain brook.

For a time Haji listened to them. It was usually possible to hear Majda Koom's kalouk from the hilltop, even when the elephant was as far as two miles away. But Haji could not hear it now. That puzzled and frightened him.

"Something is wrong?" asked Ket Kay anxiously.

"Always before I could hear the singing of Majda Koom's kalouk from the hill, but not this morning. He has gone far. We must hurry."

Once again Haji took the lead. He picked up the trail of his elephant and followed it down a gentle slope toward the valley where thick kaing grass grew in the nullah.

Haji suddenly stopped short. "Awah!" he exclaimed in dismay. "It has happened! Here is where he heard the calling of the wild ones."

"How can you know that?" asked Ket Kay.

"Majda Koom always likes to go down into this valley to eat the tall kaing grass. But here his trail turns away. From here he is heading into the thick of the jungle where there is little for him to eat. Only one thing could make him forget his hunger and turn away so sharply— the calling of the wild elephants."

"It must be as you say," agreed Ket Kay in a hushed voice. "But can their calling be heard this far away if they were on the other side of the river?"

It was a question that troubled Haji, too. In the stillness of night there was no telling how far the calling of the wild ones could be heard. Yet it seemed more likely that they had crossed over the river and were now on this side and only a few miles away.

Haji broke into a swift mile-eating trot. There was no time to lose if they were to stop Majda Koom before he reached the wild elephant herd.

In the lowlands the tracks of his elephant led them into the thick of the jungle—a world of greenish twilight where the tangle of vines and creepers and the leaves of tall trees blocked out the sky, sunlight breaking through here and there in brilliant streamers of light.

For a time Haji and Ket Kay followed a narrow game trail, one commonly used by sambur deer and wild pigs. Jungle fowl, the small wild chickens of Burma, could be heard cackling and clucking unseen in the thickets on either side of the trail.

Skirting a muddy pond, they climbed up a slippery bank and soon came out into the dazzling sunlight of open country again.

Their fast pace was beginning to tell on Ket Kay. "Haji, please wait!" he cried, gasping for air. "If we could rest a little, I would soon find my breath again."

Haji stopped and slowly came back. He realized now that taking his young friend along had been a serious mistake. Yet he could not leave him behind. "Only for a little then," he said. "Majda Koom is still far ahead or I would hear the singing of his kalouk."

Ket Kay sank down on a tussock of grass and took several deep breaths. "How can Majda Koom travel so far with his front legs chained together?" he asked.

"Hobbled elephants can go almost as fast as a man can run."

All at once Haji stiffened. He sniffed the air. He looked this way and that. Something within him had triggered a warning.

Like all who lived with the dangers of the jungle, Haji's senses had been sharpened by experience and were almost as highly developed as those of the beasts of the jungle. Every vagrant scent, every whispered sound had meaning for him.

He had the uneasy feeling that something was different, but what it was he could not tell. He had almost decided that his imagination was playing tricks on him when a slight shift in the morning breeze brought a familiar scent, one he recognized at once.

Leaning over, he touched Ket Kay on the shoulder and whispered in his ear. "I smell smoke."

Ket Kay looked puzzled. "Could it be one of the oozies?"

Haji shook his head. "They have no time for campfires when they look for their elephants."

The breeze seemed to be coming from the direction of a small grove of flame-of-the-forest trees, their tops crowned with brilliant red blossoms.

The campfire was probably that of a Karen peddler, Haji decided. Such peddlers, offering for sale their pots and pans and trinkets and spices, often traveled from elephant camp to elephant camp, and from village to village in the Valley of Ten Villages.

32

"Could it be a dacoit?" asked Ket Kay in a whisper. "There was talk at the fire last night about dacoits. It is said that they make trouble again in the north."

Haji had heard such talk from a Karen peddler who had been robbed of his money. The dacoits were outlaws; sneak thieves and robbers who sometimes banded together to make trouble. But were dacoits now coming down from the north? Haji decided to find out.

"Stay here and rest," he whispered to Ket Kay.

Crouching low, he moved swiftly and silently across a lowland bog of tussocks and little hollows. Frogs leaped from his path as he waded cautiously through a shallow marsh.

He had almost reached the stand of trees when he saw wisps of smoke curling and rising through the dark lacing of branches. The fire was closer to this side of the grove than he had thought.

Dropping to his hands and knees he quickly took cover behind a thorny clump of bushes. He moved quickly to the far side of the bushes. For a time he studied the grove, only a few yards ahead. At the edge of the grove was a thick growth of underbrush behind which he could hide, and he made for it on hands and knees.

After reaching the shade of the flame trees he rested a few moments, listened, heard the crackling of a fire, then voices—a loud, angry voice answered by a softer one. There were at least two at the fire. To Haji that meant that

33

the campers were probably not Karen peddlers, for peddlers usually traveled alone.

Haji's heart began hammering and he held his breath as he began inching closer. Little by little he picked his way through thorny underbrush until at last he could see the men by the fire through a thin screen of leaves and branches.

There were three. To his surprise, two were dressed in loose, floppy, sand-brown clothing, a fashion he had never seen before. They wore loose jackets, long trousers, hats that looked like small upside-down pots, and very strange cloth shoes.

The other, who was looking after the fire and eating boiled rice from a square of banana leaf, had the dirty, ragged look of a dacoit. He had no shoes. His loincloth and turban were a dusty black, and there was an ugly scar running down from one corner of his mouth.

The two in brown were having an angry argument in a language Haji could not understand. One finally rose to his feet and picked up a large, heavy-looking rifle.

It was then that Haji almost forgot to breathe, for lying close to where the man had been sitting were two long tusks of ivory, their heavy ends dark with dried blood. He had stumbled into a camp of the most feared and most hated outlaws of the jungle: the ivory hunters, men who killed elephants for their valuable ivory tusks.

Turning to the dacoit, the man with the gun spoke in the language of Burma. "Come," he said. "We are ready for more hunting."

"Fools!" cried the dacoit. "Have I not told you to wait? Now oozies are everywhere in the jungle. They would hear your shooting and come quickly. But late in the day when they go back to camp—then hunting will be safe. Then we can spend half the night cutting out tusks and carrying them back to our boat. Then . . ."

Haji stiffened as he heard a thrashing in the underbrush some distance behind him.

The men at the fire leaped to their feet and turned to stare in his direction.

"What was that?" asked the man with the gun.

Haji held his breath. He dared not move a muscle, for he knew, without looking back, that Ket Kay was there somewhere in the underbrush behind him.

4

Charge of the Wild Elephants

"There!" cried the man with the gun. "Something is moving!"

He raised his gun and took aim. Haji flattened himself against the ground and closed his eyes.

"No! Don't shoot!" shouted the dacoit. "The oozies would hear, and they would come!"

Haji heard a rustling sound behind him. Then something passed to his left. It must have come out into the open, for the dacoit pointed to it.

"A porcupine!" he cried. He slapped his thigh and almost doubled up with laughter.

The others looked foolish. They grumbled and took their seats again.

36

Haji slowly let out his breath. He felt so weak his head sank and, for a time, he lay there with one cheek resting against the twigs and wet leaves beneath him.

He knew what had happened. Ket Kay had followed and in his clumsy haste had stumbled in the underbrush. The noise had frightened a porcupine into the open.

It was plain that the ivory hunters knew little about wild animals. Had they been wise to the ways of the jungle, they would have known that the crashing sound in the underbrush could not have been made by so small an animal as a porcupine.

The two brown hunters soon started quarreling again. When they raised their voices in anger, Haji began his retreat. Slowly, inch by inch, he made his way back until he reached the thick underbrush at the edge of the grove.

There, as he had expected, he found Ket Kay lying half-hidden among the thorny branches, his face almost white, his big eyes round with fear. Haji covered his friend's mouth with a hand, and then, working swiftly, helped free him from the tangle that held him prisoner.

Moments later they were crawling swiftly back over the moist tussocks and into the sedge grass. A large white egret took wing in alarm as they waded the marshy brink of the swamp—and then they were running.

They did not stop until they were well into the uplands again and back on the trail of Majda Koom. When at last they paused for breath, Ket Kay wiped the tears from his eyes.

"My coming with you has made trouble, Haji. I am sorry. I wish I could be as brave and wise as you."

"But why did you follow when I told you to stay?"

Ket Kay lowered his face in shame. "I—I heard a noise. I thought it was a tiger. Fear struck at me like a spear, and I ran."

Haji pressed his lips together. There was nothing he could say, for he knew that in the jungle fear could drive a person to do strange things.

Turning, he continued in silence along the trail left by his elephant. It crossed an open meadowland where flowers—pink and white—were blooming on every bush, and giant butterflies were fluttering from blossom to blossom.

At the top of a stony ridge Haji held up his hand for silence. He listened. He could hear the screeching of brilliant green parakeets as they flew in a flock overhead, and the soft gentle cooing of doves. Suddenly he began to smile, for quite clearly now, he could hear the sweetest singing that ever an oozie could know—the singing of his elephant's kalouk. He guessed that Majda Koom was probably not more than a mile away.

"I hear him now," he told Ket Kay. "It may be that we will see him when we reach the top of that hill with the high red cliffs."

They had not gone far when Haji suddenly stopped. On the ground before him he saw the tracks of many elephants, so many that the tracks of Majda Koom could no longer be seen.

Haji's heart sank. "Wild elephants," he said, trying to hide his disappointment. "They must have crossed over the river by night. Here they joined Majda Koom."

"Awah!" cried Ket Kay. "Are we too late?" he asked anxiously. "Is there nothing we can do?"

"An oozie must always follow his elephant."

"Thakin Jensen was wrong to let Majda Koom go free," said Ket Kay. "Did he not know that Majda Koom would run away with the wild ones?"

Haji shook his head. "The thakin is wise, and he knows the ways of an elephant. He knows the love Majda Koom has for me. He believes Majda Koom would not run away from me to be with the wild ones."

"Why then did he keep Majda Koom tied to a tree all these days?"

Haji took a deep breath. There was so much to

explain that he hardly knew what to say. "The thakin did not want the wild ones close to camp. He hoped they would soon go away if Majda Koom did not come to their calling."

That was as much as Haji had time to explain as he hurried along the trail of the wild elephant herd. But he well understood the danger of having a large herd of wild ones so close to camp. The big bulls of the wild elephant herd were known to attack the tame bulls whenever they found them feeding by night in the jungle, and in such battles the tame bulls, unable to move as quickly because of the hobbles on their front legs, were often killed.

There was another danger, too, which Haji might have explained had there been time. It was known that ivory hunters often trailed the wild elephant herds about, wherever they went. And when the wild ones came close to a camp there was always a chance that ivory hunters were not far behind. These outlaws were quick to shoot any elephant they could find, whether tame or wild, for its ivory tusks.

The wild elephants had made a trail that was as easy to follow as a jungle road made by bullock carts. Every blade of grass, every stem, every bush and blossom, and every sapling had been crushed and trampled into the earth under the giant pads of a hundred or more wild elephants.

Haji knew the ivory hunters would be following that trail in a few hours. And if they discovered Majda Koom among the wild ones, they would certainly be attracted by his magnificent ivory tusks and shoot him if they could.

The thought so frightened Haji that he tried to run even faster. Somehow he had to get Majda Koom away from the rest of the herd, and do it quickly before the ivory hunters came. But exactly how this was to be done, he did not know.

The trail dipped and turned right and crossed over a flatland thickly covered with bracken ferns, ferns that reached up to the level of Haji's chin. But the ferns were soon left behind as the trail led up a gentle slope dotted with large trees.

Haji had just about passed a giant pine when he noticed the stones neatly piled under it. He stopped, waited for Ket Kay, then began searching the ground about him.

"What is it?" asked Ket Kay. "You are looking for something?"

"A stone," whispered Haji.

"A stone!" cried Ket Kay. "But why?"

Haji pointed. "To put under that tree."

Ket Kay looked at the tree and at the pile of stones, and his eyes grew big with wonder. "Awah!" he exclaimed in a whisper. "The tree is the home of a nat. Is it not so?"

Haji nodded. He looked up into the deep shadows of the pine as if expecting to see some hairy monster lurking there, though he knew full well that the evil nat spirits of the jungle were invisible.

"There has been talk in our village of such trees," whispered Ket Kay in awe. "But never before have I seen one."

Those who lived in the jungle knew very well that to pass such a tree without leaving a gift—at least a stick or stone or flower—would anger the nat spirit that lived there. And an angry nat had the power to do great harm.

Haji was not taking chances. He found two round stones of good size and placed them gingerly on top of the pile where the nat would be sure to see them. Then he hurried on, up the shady side of a rocky slope.

The climb was steep, so steep that he and Ket Kay had to pause several times for breath. As they reached the top they came to the red sandstone cliffs that towered above them like the crumbling walls of an ancient castle. There were deep cracks in the cliffs, and caves, and vines and small bushes struggling for life on tiny ledges.

From deep within one of the caves came the faint trickling sound of water, and from high above came the screech of an eagle as it spread its great wings and sprang into the air, disturbed from its nest on a rocky ledge. But the sound Haji listened for, turning his head this way and that, was the clicking and clacking of Majda Koom's wooden bell.

For a time he heard nothing. But this did not surprise him, for the morning sun was well up now and wild elephants normally rested during the heat of the day.

"They went that way," whispered Ket Kay, pointing

to the trail where the elephants had turned left and followed along the top of the ridge.

Haji held up his hand for silence. The elephants were close by, very close, of that he felt sure, and he knew the danger of going on without knowing exactly where they were.

The first great lesson an oozie learned was the value of patience, and Haji had learned that lesson well. He waited and waited, then waited some more; and presently it came—loud and clear—the sweet singing of his elephant's kalouk. From the sound of it, Majda Koom could not have been much more than a stone's throw away.

"Can you see him?" asked Ket Kay in a whisper.

"Those trees down there are in the way."

For several long moments Haji watched the treetops on the slope below. The leaves were stirring a little and seemed to be swaying in his direction. Yet he could not be sure. He began to sniff the air anxiously.

Ket Kay soon became impatient. "Why do we stand here?"

Frowning, Haji again held up his hand for silence and continued sniffing. Seconds later he was finally rewarded with the good spicy smell of crushed grass, which he knew so well. It was the smell given off by elephants.

Haji relaxed a little and took a deep breath. "The wind is right," he whispered to Ket Kay. "It blows from the elephants to us. I smell them."

43

"That is good?"

Haji nodded. "A wind from us to the elephants would be dangerous. It would carry our scent to them. They might charge us or run away if they could smell us."

"What do we do now?"

"First I have to find out if Majda Koom is alone or with the wild ones. I will follow their trail far enough so I can look down at them. Wait here for me."

Ket Kay caught his breath. "No, no, Haji! Please! Do not leave me again."

"Here you are safe," Haji explained, trying to calm his fears. "Here you can hide in a cave until I come back for you."

Ket Kay looked into the shadowy depth of a nearby cave and shrank back as if he sensed some unseen beast crouching there. "No! Fear would strike at me again and—and I would come running."

There was just enough truth in what he said to make Haji wonder if it might not be more dangerous to leave him behind than to take him along.

"Please, Haji," Ket Kay begged. "I can be quiet. I will do as you say."

Haji knew it was useless to argue further. Frowning darkly, he began advancing slowly along the ridge, following the trail made by the elephants, with Ket Kay close at his heels.

They soon passed the place where the elephants had turned down the slope. As they continued along the top

44

of the hill, the stand of trees between them and the herd began thinning out. Here and there, through openings between the leaves, Haji caught glimpses of the herd below.

Only a few more steps would bring them clear of the trees and give them a view of the whole herd. Haji dropped to his hands and knees and began crawling, knowing that the bushes and tall grass would hide him from view.

He suddenly realized he was following an old drag path. It reminded him of that day when Majda Koom had dragged a huge teak log over this very path on the way to the river. As he continued slowly along he tried to remember the details of the jungle around him, and to make a picture in his mind of the place where the elephants were resting.

He knew one thing for certain—the slope down which the elephants had gone was not a steep one, nor would it take them long to charge up the hill if they knew he and Ket Kay were there. One careless step, even the snap of a twig, could be enough to frighten them into attack.

The sleepy morning peace of the jungle was suddenly broken by the angry grunting and coughing of long-tailed monkeys. Haji caught in his breath, listened, every muscle in his body straining with tension.

For a few moments he heard nothing more. Then came the sharp call of a barking deer, sounding a warning. The deer and the monkeys were somewhere high on a wooded slope some distance beyond the elephants.

Haji dropped to the ground and lay perfectly still, for the wild ones were fully alerted now, and the big bulls were trumpeting their alarm, warning the unseen enemy not to come closer.

The elephants, as well as Haji, knew that the warning calls of the monkeys and deer meant that one of the big cats were prowling nearby. The monkeys had seen one of their most hated enemies—either a tiger or a leopard—and had sounded the alarm. Their warning may have saved the life of the barking deer.

Presently, but much fainter now, came another chorus of angry grunts, this time from the top of the ridge

and far to the right. The big cat was moving off in that direction. It must have gone over the crest of the hill and into the valley beyond, for neither the monkeys nor the barking deer sounded their alarm again.

Haji waited for some time to allow the elephants to quiet down again before going on. Signaling Ket Kay to follow, he crawled ahead and took cover behind a shoulder-high thicket of bushes. Then rising slowly to his feet, he looked down on one of the largest herds of wild elephants he had ever seen.

There were large bulls and cows, and young ones of all sizes—and one little one, not more than a week old, standing for protection between the front legs of its mother.

The elephants were gathered below the slope on a flat, sandy wash that Haji remembered had once been the bed of a river, before it had changed its course. A small winding stream of fresh water flowed through it, forming shallow pools here and there, from which some of the elephants were drinking.

Others were standing quietly, switching their tails and flopping their big ears to drive off the flies. Still others were sucking up sand in their trunks and blowing it over their backs to protect themselves from the burning rays of the sun.

Haji frowned. If some of the wild ones were already finding the heat of the sun uncomfortable, the herd would soon be moving again, into the deep shade of the jungle where it would be nearly impossible to find Majda Koom without alarming the rest of the herd.

Majda Koom should have been easy to spot, being so much larger than any of the other bulls. But Haji was unable to find him.

Could it be that Majda Koom was off somewhere by himself? That was not difficult to believe. The big bulls often strayed some distance from the herd. Yet the singing of Majda Koom's bell, the only time they had heard it, meant that he could not be far away. Majda Koom had to be found quickly. But how?

Dropping to his hands and knees again, he crawled swiftly along the drag path until he came to a shelf of rock that curved out high over the slope. The far end of it, he knew, would give him a good look at the entire herd.

To get out there meant crawling out along the edge of a cliff where there wasn't a bush or vine or even a blade of grass to keep him from being seen by the elephants. But that was a risk he was willing to take, knowing that elephants had poor eyesight and could not see very well at a distance. They depended rather upon their keen sense of smell and hearing for protection.

He had crawled almost halfway out on the rock shelf when he heard Ket Kay following close behind him. He turned, shook his head, and signaled for him to go back.

Ket Kay became frightened. He turned and, in his haste to scramble back to cover behind the bushes, struck a loose stone with his foot.

Haji watched in horror as it slid to the very edge of the rock shelf, balanced there for a split second, then dropped out of sight. He heard it crash on the rocks below and go clattering down the slope.

Instantly one of the big bulls sounded the alarm by hitting the ground with his trunk. It made a hollow, ringing sound, like striking a metal pipe with a hammer.

Every elephant wheeled to face the direction from which the sound had come, their heads raised as they spread out their ears like giant fans.

Haji dared not move a muscle, for all the elephants seemed to be staring directly at him.

The sight was too much for Ket Kay. He let out a yell as he sprang to his feet.

"They see us!" he screamed.

It was all the elephants needed. Bellowing with rage, they made for the slope in a mighty charge.

"Run!" yelled Haji. "Back to the caves!"

Ket Kay needed no urging now. He dashed away at top speed. But fast as he was, Ket Kay was no match for the speed of the charging elephants. Haji realized it was too late.

5

Jungle Terror

Haji stood frozen at the edge of the cliff, watching helplessly as the gray tide of angry beasts came thundering over the sand flats. It was like watching something in a dream. He couldn't think. He couldn't move.

The charging elephants seemed to be headed for a place on the towpath ahead of Ket Kay. They would soon be blocking his way, cutting off his retreat before he could reach the safety of the caves.

Just as the elephants reached the slope Haji suddenly came alive. There was only one way to save Ket Kay now. That was to attract the elephants to himself, to draw them off in another direction.

He began screaming. He jumped up and down,

waving his arms. He grabbed up loose stones and flung them down on the rocks below.

The elephants heard him. They swerved in his direction.

He ran back along the cliff to the towpath. He kept yelling and throwing stones all the while as they came rushing up the slope.

He waited until they were close enough to see him clearly. Then he turned and ran, leading them farther along the towpath, away from the caves and Ket Kay.

On they came in a mighty rush. They were gaining so rapidly he could almost feel the breath of their angry snortings. Though he ran as he had never run before, he knew he could not keep up the pace for long.

With only seconds to spare, he plunged down through the thickest of the jungle on the back side of the slope. He dodged around trees and boulders. He dashed through thickets of thorny brush that stabbed at his flesh like hot needles.

He was beginning to tire now. But he forced himself on, dropping down over a rocky ledge and into more thickets.

All he needed was enough time to hide without being seen, and he had one thing in his favor—he knew elephants. He knew that charging elephants were in the habit of closing their eyes to protect them when rushing through thick brush. He also knew that elephants, because of their tremendous weight, were usually forced to check their speed a little when charging downhill. They were still close behind him, but no longer gaining.

Yet he could not keep ahead of them much longer. The desperate race had used up most of his strength. His legs felt rubbery beneath him.

He stumbled, caught his balance and went on, and stumbled again. His eyes were blurring. His breath was coming in screaming gasps.

At last he found what he was looking for—a giant pine, with a massive trunk and a wide skirt of branches that almost touched the ground.

He stumbled behind it, crawling under the cover of its branches. There, behind the trunk of the tree, he made himself as small as he could, and waited.

Seconds later the elephants came by in a mighty avalanche of bone and muscle. The thunder and crashing of their big pads made the earth quiver and quake beneath him.

Branches on both sides of the tree were shattered and swept aside as the beasts plunged on in an endless stream.

Haji was pelted with showers of sand and pebbles and broken twigs from the churning pads. But he was already feeling better. He had found his breath again and could breathe deeply.

By now the leaders had lost his scent and could no longer see him or hear him ahead of them. He knew they would not turn back to search for him. That was not the way of charging elephants.

Their only purpose was to protect the herd. Once they had passed the thing they were chasing, the thing that had threatened them, whether man or one of the big

cats, they would keep rushing on to put danger far behind them.

It wasn't long before the herd began thinning out. At the tail end came the young ones—two, three, and four years of age—and behind them came one large elephant. That seemed unusual.

Why would a fully grown elephant be the last of the herd? Could it possibly be Majda Koom? Haji did not think so. Looking out from under the branches to make certain, he saw one of the rarest sights in the world of wild animals. It was a large cow carrying her newly born baby in her trunk.

As the rumbling and trumpeting of the wild ones slowly faded away in the distance, Haji stretched out on the cool damp ground and rested his aching muscles for a few minutes before starting back up the slope.

Majda Koom was up there somewhere. Of that he felt certain. Any tame elephant as big and powerful as Majda Koom had little to fear in the jungle, and was not easily frightened. Not only that, but he had been somewhere beyond the far end of the herd when the charge began, and his front legs were chained together. He could not possibly have kept up for long with the mad rush of the wild ones.

Haji had not climbed very far up the slope before he heard once again the sweet music of his elephant's kalouk.

His answer was a joyful cry that burst from his throat like a song. "I come, big brother! I come!"

A good oozie always took care to tell his elephant of his coming while still some distance away. Even before he reached the crest of the hill he could hear the flopping of elephant ears, and the tearing and crunching and blowing sounds of a feeding elephant.

He sang out again. "I come! I come! Your oozie comes for you."

Then singing and laughing loudly to let out all the tight feelings bottled up within him, he broke through the last of the underbrush and came out on the open towpath.

There in the morning sunlight, less than two stone throws away, stood the mighty Majda Koom, his head high, his ears spread out like enormous fans. Seeing him again made Haji so happy he felt like running up and throwing his arms around the big one's trunk. But he knew better.

When feeding alone in the jungle, a tame elephant had to look out for himself and be his own master. He had to decide who was friend and who was foe, and he looked with suspicion upon every man or beast he happened to meet.

Haji knew very well he had to keep his distance until Majda Koom recognized him. Since elephants lived slow-motion lives and were rarely in a hurry about anything, that could take quite a while.

"Why do you stand there and stare?" he asked, laughing, although he knew he was too far away for Majda Koom to recognize him by sight. "You know who I am. It is I, Haji."

Slowly he went several steps closer, sat down in a patch of sunlight, and waited. The big bull lifted his trunk almost straight above him and waved it back and forth, back and forth, like the swaying dance of a cobra to a snake-charmer's piping. But he could not catch Haji's scent.

Although still not close enough to be recognized by sight, Haji knew he could prove his identity through his actions and by the sound of his voice.

"Lah! Lah! Lah! Come on! Come on! Come on!" he cried.

His elephant paid no attention. Flopping his big ears, he half-turned away and began breaking off small leafy branches with his trunk and stuffing them into his mouth.

"How can you be hungry after eating all night?" asked Haji. He had to keep talking. What he said made little difference. The constant droning of his voice would have a soothing effect on his elephant.

"Look at the sun, big brother. See how high it is in the sky. Must I wait here all day watching you eat when I have not yet had one bite of breakfast?"

Majda Koom turned away. He took several steps down the towpath only to pause again and start ripping off branches from other trees.

Haji laughed loud enough for his elephant to hear. He could tell now that he had been recognized. But the big bull had been chained to a tree for so long that he wanted to enjoy a few more moments of liberty before going back with his oozie.

Respecting the wishes of his elephant, Haji waited a little longer. Then, changing to words of command, he cried sharply, "Digo lah! Digo lah! Come here! Come here!"

Slowly Majda Koom turned to face him, took several steps forward and stopped. It was his way of saying he was ready, that he recognized Haji as his master.

"Hmit! Get down!" ordered Haji in a firm voice.

Obediently, Majda Koom got to his knees with his hind legs, then lowered his great body to the ground, with his front legs straight out before him.

Walking up to him swiftly, Haji gave him a friendly pat on the trunk, took the chain off his forelegs and climbed onto his head.

"Tah! Stand up!" he cried.

Moments later, bobbing and swaying to the big easy steps of his elephant, Haji followed the towpath that led to the caves.

As they approached the crumbling red cliffs he sang out at the top of his voice, "All is well, Ket Kay! I am riding Majda Koom! We come for you!"

The caves suddenly came into view. Haji looked at them closely, expecting his friend to pop out of one of them and come running. But Ket Kay did not come out.

Haji called again as Majda Koom stopped in front of the largest of the caves. Still no answer. Had fear driven Ket Kay so far back into a cave that he could hear nothing from the outside?

Sliding down the face of his elephant, Haji caught

hold of a tusk and swung lightly to the ground. He ran into the cave and called out again. Only the ringing echoes of his own voice came back to him, and with it the faint trickle and gurgle of running water.

This could be one of those caves that went on and on endlessly, Haji decided, and he continued on, feeling his way carefully around a sharp bend that cut off daylight from the cave's entrance.

Now he found himself in almost complete darkness. He suddenly remembered how Ket Kay stayed close to the campfires on dark nights. Had his fear of the wild elephants been so great it had driven him into the darkest reaches of the cave?

Haji did not know. He could only be certain of one thing—that this cave was the one he himself would have chosen had he been in Ket Kay's place. It was large enough to run into without bending over, yet small enough to prevent an elephant from following. The other caves, much smaller, could not have been entered easily, even on hands and knees.

"Ket Kay!" he shouted again. "Answer me, Ket Kay!"

Again no answer. He went on, deeper and deeper into the black nothingness before him. The gurgle of running water grew louder, and the walls of rough rock became wet to his touch.

Presently the cave slanted sharply downward. He was soon walking in cool water that became deeper with every step. Convinced at last that Ket Kay could not have gone that way, he gave one last shout and turned back.

With growing alarm he began searching the other caves. The hissing of a small animal warned him away from the first. As he crawled into another he found the air so heavy with unpleasant smells he could hardly breathe. The narrow cave entrance opened up into a large chamber which suddenly came alive with soft rustlings and squeakings. Looking up, he saw many large bats hanging from the ceiling.

Haji almost fell over himself in his haste to get out. He had heard it said that the evil nat spirits of the jungle often turned themselves into bats. To see so many in one place, he felt, was an unlucky sign—a sign that something very bad had happened to Ket Kay.

Anxiously he searched the other small caves one by one, finding nothing. But if Ket Kay was not in the caves, what had happened to him? Where could he be?

Running to Majda Koom, standing quietly in the shade nearby, Haji tugged at one of his big ears. "Come, big brother."

With the elephant lumbering along at his heels, he began backtracking, following the trail over which he and Ket Kay had come only a short time before. He moved slowly down the slope, searching for some sign of Ket Kay's footprints. He had little hope of seeing any, for the trail had been flattened and hardened by the herd of wild elephants. Yet it seemed reasonable that if Ket Kay had not stopped at the caves, he must have run right past them and headed back for camp.

Now and then Haji paused to call out Ket Kay's

name. He reached the bottom of the hill, crossed over the lowlands of tall ferns, and was about to start up the slope to the next ridge when he stopped and called out again.

Faintly an answering cry came back to him. Or was it merely his echo? He called again, and yet again, but heard nothing more.

Bitterly discouraged, suddenly feeling very hot and very tired, he was about to begin the steep climb when he happened to notice Majda Koom.

The big elephant bull was standing alert, his head high, his big ears spread out. His attention seemed to be fixed on something higher up the slope. Majda Koom had heard the sound, too!

Haji's heart hammered wildly with new hope. He lifted his arms, his wordless command to be picked up. The elephant's trunk slipped about his waist, tightened, and moments later he was riding swiftly up the trail on the head of Majda Koom.

The faint cry had sounded like that of a human voice. Yet Haji felt uncertain. If it really was Ket Kay who had cried out, why hadn't he answered when called again?

Majda Koom was now approaching the top of the ridge. Filling his lungs, Haji shouted, "Ket Kay! Answer me!"

He heard nothing. There was no sound but the soft bubbling noises of some jade-green pigeons feeding on the trail ahead.

A breeze had sprung up, and Majda Koom tested it

by holding his trunk high and moving it back and forth. He seemed to sense that Haji was searching for someone and was doing his best to help. He moved a few steps more up the trail and tested the air again. This time he turned to face some large trees off to the left. The breeze was blowing from that direction. Had he caught the scent?

"Ket Kay, can you hear me?" shouted Haji.

Majda Koom's ears suddenly snapped out wide as a faint sound came back to them. It sounded almost like a low moan. Haji drew in his breath and held it so long it hurt. If Ket Kay had made the sound, something terrible must have happened to him.

"I come, Ket Kay. Where are you?"

A wild scream of terror came from the trees. It stabbed through Haji like a knife. Quickly he pushed against the backs of his elephant's ears with both feet. It was his signal to go ahead. Majda Koom breasted his way through the green tangle of vines and underbrush. Small trees cracked and fell before him.

"No!" screamed a voice that sounded like Ket Kay's. "Go back! Leave me alone!"

Haji could hardly believe his ears. Had Ket Kay gone out of his mind? "Do not be afraid," he yelled. "It is I myself, Haji, who comes for you."

"No!" screeched the voice. "Come no closer! I know—" his voice broke in a sob. "I know you are not Haji. I—I know *what* you are. Haji is dead!"

Haji was too stunned to speak. The power of fear in the jungle was a terrible thing, he knew. He leaned back, bringing his elephant to a halt. Ket Kay needed time to understand that no danger threatened him.

"I come no closer, Ket Kay," said Haji in as calm a voice as he could manage. "Please believe me. You have nothing to fear. I am not a ghost. I am not of the spirit world. I did not die. Spirits do not walk abroad in the light of day. You hear my voice and you know it is I, Haji, who speaks to you."

"No, no, no. Go away, go away." Ket Kay began sobbing aloud.

Tears stung Haji's eyes. Fear had driven his friend to the edge of madness, and there was little he could do to help him.

He waited patiently, hoping that the passing of time would quiet his friend's fears. Majda Koom began feeling around with the tip of his trunk, feeding on bits of tempting greenery within reach.

Every now and then Haji pressed his feet for an instant against the big ears. Majda Koom responded by taking a step or two forward, only to pause again and eat some more. Ket Kay's sobbing could scarcely be heard above the ripping and tearing and crunching sounds of the feeding elephant.

Haji laughed softly, yet loud enough for his friend to hear. "Majda Koom never stops eating," he said, chuckling. "Look at him, Ket Kay. He has eaten all night, and

63

now he is eating again. You can see there is nothing wrong with his appetite. He did not die. He is not of the spirit world."

Ket Kay stopped sobbing. "Is—is it really you, Haji?" he asked timidly.

"You know me, Ket Kay. Come to us. We wait to take you home."

After a long pause Ket Kay said, "My leg hurts. Something is wrong with it."

"Then let us come to you," said Haji. Pushing through the underbrush he found Ket Kay perched on a low branch, his right leg hanging, the ankle badly swollen.

With Majda Koom's help he was soon seated on the elephant's head where Haji could steady him with his arms.

Ket Kay began sobbing again as they headed back toward camp. "I—I heard you screaming, Haji. I—I thought—"

"I was screaming to get the elephants' attention," explained Haji. "You can see nothing happened to me."

When they finally reached camp the sun stood overhead in the noonday sky. Someone saw them coming and gave a shout. People came running, shouting questions. But Haji did not stop until he came to the high veranda of the thakin's new house.

Thakin Jensen himself came out, a pipe clamped firmly between his teeth. "It's good you're back. We had expected you long ago."

Haji swallowed. "Please, Thakin, help Ket Kay. He has hurt his leg."

Ket Kay was quickly carried inside where the thakin could look after him. Haji waited beside his elephant. A crowd gathered and Oo Yan, chief of the oozies, came up in his spotless white coat. He listened in silence as Haji told what had happened.

"You did well," said Oo Yan. He shook his head. "But do not expect the red-faced one to be pleased. He looks only for some excuse to say you are too young to be an oozie."

Haji had a sinking feeling. "How can you know that?" he asked.

"Already he complains about you. He has said a good oozie would have brought back Majda Koom hours ago."

At that moment Thakin Jensen came out. "It seems to be only a sprained ankle," he said. "The boy should be up and about in two or three days."

The red-faced inspector suddenly appeared at the doorway. "I say again that he is responsible for this boy's injury."

The thakin looked troubled. He took the pipe from his mouth and said, "Inspector, I should like to suggest that we hear what Haji has to say before we decide—"

"Before *we* decide!" snorted the inspector angrily. "Let me remind you, Jensen, that I am in command here. I make the decisions, and I have heard enough. He took an inexperienced playmate along as if he were going on a picnic! No wonder he was late! It's the most childish thing I've ever heard of."

"A mistake, I grant you," answered the thakin quietly. "But one he's not likely to make again."

"He'll not have a chance!" roared the inspector. "Send him to help train the young ones at the elephant school. That's an order, Jensen. Meanwhile, I intend to search for an experienced oozie worthy of this great beast."

6

An Outlaw Returns

The red-faced inspector had been gone two days when Haji was called to the house of Thakin Jensen. He found the thakin seated behind a small table on the shaded veranda, with Oo Yan standing nearby.

The thakin wasted no time. "You heard the inspector's orders the other day, did you not?" he asked.

Haji nodded, hoping that by some miracle the orders had been changed.

Picking up a paper the thakin said, "The inspector put those orders in writing before he left. He wanted it clearly understood that you are no longer to be the oozie of Majda Koom."

Haji swallowed and nodded again. For the last two

days he had hardly slept or eaten a bite, haunted by the helpless, hopeless feeling those orders had given him.

Thakin Jensen puffed thoughtfully on his pipe for a moment. "I know how much Majda Koom means to you, Haji, and I'm sorry, truly sorry."

"The fault was not yours, Haji," said Oo Yan softly. "It was the will of the gods. Remember that. If the gods had not willed it to happen, it would not have happened."

"Yes," said the thakin. "What we cannot change, we must accept. But this much I can promise you, Haji. You shall have first pick of the young ones at the elephant school, and you will train him and care for him and in time become his oozie."

Haji stared. Didn't the thakin understand that the great elephant being taken from him was all that mattered? Had anyone ever seen an elephant half so magnificent? Would the world ever see his like again? Haji wet his lips. "But—but what about Majda Koom?"

The thakin cleared his throat. "We know the great love he has for you. We know also that he recognizes only you as his master. We can only hope he is not too old to be trained to accept the orders of other oozies. It will not be easy. That we know. It will take time, and we will need your help."

Haji could only nod. No matter how much it hurt, he would help so long as Majda Koom was treated with kindness and patience.

"Very well then." Thakin Jensen stood up. "You will look after Majda Koom until his new oozie arrives."

Until his new oozie arrives . . . Until his new oozie arrives . . . The words kept echoing over and over again in Haji's head as he walked away. Beyond the royal palms he came to a stop at the edge of the river. A tree floated by, far out in the middle, and on its trunk sat a large turtle sunning itself. Haji was gazing at the tree and the turtle, hardly seeing them, when he heard a sound behind him.

Ket Kay came limping up, his young brown face stained with tears. "I hid under the thakin's house to listen. It—it was in my head that maybe the thakin would find some way to—to—" He sank to his knees and began to sob.

"The thakin is good," said Haji. "He could do nothing."

"Now there is no hoping. You have lost Majda Koom and it is on my head. The fault is mine," sobbed Ket Kay.

"The red-faced one had a part in this," said Haji gently.

Ket Kay paid no attention to him. "When my leg is strong again I will go back to live in my village in the rice valley. It is there I belong. Never again will I trouble you."

"Awah!" exclaimed Haji. "The blame is not yours. Did you not hear Oo Yan, how he said it was the will of the gods?"

Ket Kay looked up at him, slowly blinking away his tears. "But—but had I not gone with you that morning—"

"Had you not, the red-faced one would have found

some other reason for taking Majda Koom from me. All would be well with us now had he not come to camp."

A sharp squeal split the afternoon quiet. They turned in time to see a young elephant come charging at them through the palms.

"Run!" yelled Haji.

Ket Kay went limping off at a slow trot.

Haji held his ground until the elephant was almost upon him. Then he leaped nimbly to one side. The elephant turned, but not before Haji had dodged behind the nearest palm tree.

"Wah! So you want to chase people and have fun, do you?" said Haji, dashing off to another palm tree.

The young elephant followed, squealing and snorting. But it was not quick enough in the turning and darting and dodging to keep up with Haji.

"You must be the naughty little girl Byoo once told me about," he said, peeking at her from behind another tree.

She was not so little anymore, standing about five feet and four inches at the shoulders, a good two inches taller than Haji himself.

One of the five-year-olds who would soon be going for training and to learn some manners at the elephant school, she was just a naughty young elephant who liked to chase people. To her it was a game, but she did not realize her strength, and that made her dangerous.

Haji took no chances. If he stumbled and fell, she would be on him in an instant. And should she step on him, which she might do in her excitement, her great weight could easily crush the life from his body.

Dodging from one tree to another, Haji worked his way slowly toward the row of thatched bamboo huts on stilts where the oozies lived, huts that could only be entered by climbing up bamboo ladders.

Haji kept up the dodging and darting game until Ket Kay had reached the safety of one of the huts. Then he made a sudden dash around a tree and grabbed hold of the young elephant's tail.

Squealing with fright and anger, she began spinning around in an effort to get at him.

Haji laughed. "Now we will race. Come! Show me how fast you can run."

With that he let go of the tail and set off at top speed across the open field. The elephant, spurred on by anger, followed close on his heels.

Cheers and laughter came from a group of three oozies nearby as Haji made for the hut where Ket Kay stood watching.

"Look how the brave Haji runs from a little calf!" yelled one of the oozies, slapping his thighs and howling with laughter.

Haji put on an extra burst of speed. Reaching the hut, he swung up the ladder and out of danger with only seconds to spare.

The little elephant was not through yet. She stopped, looked this way and that, as if trying to decide what to do

next. Suddenly she spotted the oozies and made for them full tilt.

Now it was Haji's turn to laugh as the oozies took to their heels and scattered like leaves before the wind.

"What is it?" asked the woman of the hut, coming up behind Haji to look out the door. "Ayee," she said softly. "It was well Oo Yan warned us to watch our children today, with so many elephants about."

Shouts came from farther down the street. Another young elephant, probably less than four years old, was chasing a pye-dog near the cooking fires. Screams of the women frightened it off. But in its haste to get away it upset a large pot of steaming rice.

"Ayee," the woman behind Haji wailed again. "How much longer must the elephants be kept in camp?"

"Oo Yan will keep them all chained to trees till the wild herd and ivory hunters have gone far from our forests," replied Haji.

With the working elephants chained nearby, the young ones had become restless. Even the youngest wandered away from their mothers. The calves found little to do except get into trouble.

They chased each other through camp. They found it fun to run after chickens and ducks and pye-dogs. Some burned their trunks at the cooking fires. Others made nuisances of themselves by constantly begging for food from the children, who enjoyed spoiling them.

Although the five-year-olds were often rough in their play, only one of them had discovered the fun of chasing people. Haji's closest friend, Byoo, again spoke of the calf that night at the campfire.

"It must be the one that chased you," he told Haji. "A little female. I have been watching her for over a year now, and I have a good name for her already—Tah Sin Ma—Miss Wild Elephant."

Haji looked surprised. No one had the right to name a young elephant except the boy who was to train it and become its oozie at the elephant school. "This is the calf you want for yourself?" he asked.

"I will take it if you do not choose it first," answered Byoo. "The thakin has made it plain that you can have first choice."

Ket Kay leaned forward. "If the choosing were mine, I would want a more gentle one. Why do you choose such a naughty one, Byoo?"

Haji smiled. "The gentle are not always the best," he explained. "Some are gentle only because they are too lazy to be naughty. I have not seen the others, but Byoo knows them well. I know that if Byoo chooses the naughty one, it will be for good reason."

"I would hear your reasons, Byoo, so I can learn more about the choosing of elephants," begged Ket Kay.

"You have only to come with me when the elephant school begins and I will show you the others, and the weak and the strong of each. The one you call naughty is bigger and stronger than the others, and she has more spirit."

That she had more spirit no one could doubt, especially after she began chasing the women away from their cooking fires the following day. The women complained. The oozies laughed and did nothing.

Another day passed. The women complained more loudly than ever, and still the oozies did nothing. That is, they did nothing until the lively calf made the mistake of chasing Oo Yan himself. That was when the thakin decided something had to be done.

"Enough is enough, Oo Yan," he said. "I want you to teach that calf to mind her manners. Unless we sweeten her temper a bit now I'm afraid she's going to be a difficult pupil at the elephant school."

To make a trap for the naughty one, Oo Yan passed a strong rope between two palms growing close together. He made a large loop at the end he had passed through and placed it carefully on the ground.

There was no problem in getting the young elephant to chase one of the oozies. He led her directly to the two palms and slipped between them. She tried to follow, but could not.

At the same instant oozies in hiding jerked the rope, and the loop tightened on one of her front legs.

For several minutes she squealed in terror, and struggled frantically to break loose.

When she quieted, Oo Yan came up with a wooden paddle, waved it in front of her, then went back and gave her a couple of good whacks on her rear end.

Again she squealed, this time in anger, kicking and

75

tugging to get at him. He showed her the paddle again, and whacked her once more.

Ket Kay looked on in amazement. "Why does he strike her?" he asked.

"To teach her better manners," answered Haji. He could well understand Ket Kay's confusion, for in the land of Burma children were always treated with kindness and patience and were never spanked by their parents.

"How can striking a young one help its manners? Do they do this in the land where the thakin comes from?" Ket Kay asked, referring to England.

"I do not know," said Haji. "The thakin could have learned this way from the elephants."

"From the elephants? Do elephants strike their young ones?"

Haji nodded. "The next time a little one goes too far from its mother, watch and see. If it does not come quickly when she calls, she will give it a blow or two with her trunk."

Now, at Oo Yan's order, other oozies who had been chased came up, one by one, to show the paddle to the naughty one and to give her a couple of taps on the rear. None of them struck with strength, for they all loved the little elephant and had no wish to hurt her.

Last of all came Haji's turn. But when the paddle was offered to him he refused it, for by then the little elephant was making small whimpering noises almost like those of a crying child.

"That's quite enough, I should think," said the thakin. "Now leave her, all of you, except for the lad who is to be her oozie."

As the oozies drifted away, Haji and Ket Kay drew back into the grove of palms to watch from a distance. Only Byoo remained behind with the little elephant. He kept petting her on the trunk, talking softly to her all the while.

Presently Byoo's mother came with a tray of bananas and balls of cooked rice—special treats all elephants love. These he fed to the calf one at a time, speaking gently, and patting her for short periods between each offering.

"When will he let her go?" asked Ket Kay.

"First she must learn to know him as a friend," answered Haji.

That did not take long. When Byoo loosened the rope snare from her leg and took it off, she followed after him, begging for the last of the balls of rice.

"Wah!" exclaimed Haji, chuckling. "She learns quickly, that one." He felt certain she had learned her lesson well and would never again make a game of chasing people.

The naughty one, of course, was only part of the problem. There could be no peace in camp so long as many young elephants were using it for a playground. But that problem simply faded away a couple of days later when the herd of wild elephants and the ivory hunters finally left the area, and the working elephants, with their young, were once again given the freedom of the jungle at night.

The days that followed, days Haji spent with Majda Koom in the jungle, would have been happy and carefree ones had he been able to forget that the new oozie would soon be coming to take the great elephant from him. He dreaded the coming of each new day, for he knew it might be the last he and Majda Koom would ever be able to enjoy together. He was up before dawn to hurry off into the jungle in search of his elephant, and usually came riding back into camp an hour or two later. After a quick breakfast of boiled rice, he would take his elephant for a morning bath in the river.

The big bull would lie on his side in a foot or two of water as Haji, often with the help of Ket Kay, scrubbed him down with wadded stems of a creeper that lathered like soap. Haji then rubbed him with a coconut shell. It was during this rubbing that Majda Koom usually lay very still, the better to enjoy the scratchy sensation it gave him.

All about them and along the edge of the river dozens of other elephants were being bathed. The children of oozies were there, too, some helping, others walking about on the sides of the elephants as if the animals were so many rounded gray stones in the river.

It was a time when oozies laughed and joked with each other as they worked, as if they had not a care in the world. But Haji did not join in their merriment. For him it was a time to give full attention to the needs of Majda

Koom, finishing the bath with a careful inspection inside the big ears for ticks and with a check of each foot for thorns and splinters.

When this was done he would quickly mount his elephant and ride off into the jungle where the new oozie, if he came, could not find them, and where they could spend the long lazy hours of the day together.

These were hours in which Haji tried to relive again the glorious days of his childhood when he, as a boy of eight or nine, had explored the wilderness for miles around with Majda Koom on the elephant resting days.

As in times gone by, they always stopped at his favorite mango tree. There Majda Koom lifted him up with his trunk so he could pick the very ripest fruit from the tree.

They would cross the river, as they had done so many times before, Majda Koom holding his trunk above the surface for air as he sank out of sight to walk along

the bottom in funny, floating, slow-motion steps. It had been during these crossings years ago that Haji had learned to swim, though he often held onto the end of the elephant's trunk for support.

Day after day they ventured again into the shade of the deep gorge where the heat of the day could not reach them. Often Haji slept for an hour or more, with Majda Koom standing over him, rocking slowly from side to side, always rocking, as elephants always do during their resting periods.

Best of all, Haji loved the hours they shared together exploring the wilderness. It was then, in those glorious hours on the head of the mighty Majda Koom, that Haji felt like the prince of all the jungle.

But those hours came to an end in the gathering shadows of late afternoon when they turned once more toward camp. Then fear came back. It tightened into a knot within him, reminding him that this could be the day that the new oozie was waiting in camp to take the elephant from him.

Day after day the fear grew in his heart. Finally there came a day when Ket Kay ran to meet him as he entered camp.

"A man has come," he said breathlessly. "He has business with the thakin now, and the thakin has sent me to find you."

The racing of Haji's heart suddenly stopped, and for a long moment he sat as if turned to stone. The new oozie had come. He was waiting. It was the end of all things.

In a voice he hardly recognized as his own, he ordered his elephant down. He hobbled him and turned him loose to feed in the jungle during the night. Then on stiff legs he made for the house of the thakin.

As he climbed the steps to the veranda, he saw the stranger, a man in clean white loincloth and white turban.

At the sound of Haji's coming the man turned to face him. Haji stopped short. He found himself staring at an ugly scar running down from a corner of the man's mouth.

He had seen that scar once before—on the face of the outlaw dacoit in the camp of the ivory hunters only a few weeks ago.

7

A New Oozie
for Majda Koom

Upon leaving the thakin's house, Haji found his friends
Byoo and Ket Kay waiting for him among the palms.

"What of the stranger?" asked Byoo. "He does not
look like an oozie. I do not trust him."

"Nor I," said Haji. "He is a dacoit—the same one I
saw in the camp of the ivory hunters."

"Awah!" cried Ket Kay. "Is a dacoit to be the new
oozie for Majda Koom?"

"That cannot be," said Byoo. "Dacoits know nothing
about elephants."

Haji nodded. "This one comes as a messenger for the
red-faced one. His letter to the thakin says that a new
oozie for Majda Koom has not yet been found."

Byoo flashed his big smile. "The red-faced one is learning," he said with a chuckle. "Good oozies are not easy to find."

Haji knew what he meant. There were many very good oozies working in the elephant camps of Burma. But these oozies had elephants of their own, whom they loved, and who loved them in return. None of them could be tempted to trade his elephant for another—no, not even for one as well known and magnificent as Majda Koom.

"Thakin Jensen says it could take many days before another oozie is found. He will wait no longer. Majda Koom is needed now on the log drags. I am to be his oozie until the new one has come."

Ket Kay gave a joyful shout. "Now you are oozie again!"

"Only for a little," answered Haji sadly. "The hot season comes in a few days."

Ket Kay looked at him closely. "Something is troubling you?"

"That dacoit," answered Haji. "Does a thief work for honest pay? It is in my head that this one came here for yet another reason."

"What other business could he have here?" asked Byoo, the smile fading from his moonlike face. "There is nothing for him to steal in the huts of the oozies, and the thakin's money box is always well guarded."

"I know," said Haji, feeling a little foolish. Strangers passed through camp every now and then, and some were

83

probably dacoits. Who could say? Yet, it did seem strange that a dacoit, who had been serving ivory hunters only a few weeks before, should suddenly appear in camp as an honest carrier of messages.

"How long will he stay?" asked Ket Kay, blinking his big eyes slowly.

"For the night only," answered Haji. "In the morning he takes back a message from the thakin to the red-faced one. It will explain why he is making me an oozie again."

News that Majda Koom was to join the other working elephants in the teak forests spread from campfire to campfire that evening. Over two years had passed since anyone had seen the giant tusker at work and the oozies spoke in hushed voices of his magnificent strength.

"In those days the largest of the logs were always left for Majda Koom," said the wrinkled one. "It was often said that he did as much work in a day as any other elephant in camp could do in three."

"It was even so," Haji said to Byoo in a whisper, for it was not polite for a boy to speak up in a gathering of his elders unless asked to do so.

"Majda Koom had the best of all oozies then," one of the oozies reminded them, speaking of Haji's father. "But can he do as well with only the boy Haji to guide him?"

The oozies murmured among themselves and several glanced in Haji's direction. The unwelcomed attention suddenly made him feel uneasy.

"It would be good to see what Majda Koom could do

84

with the big log in the sand by the black rocks," suggested one of the oozies.

"Ayee," said another. "Let Majda Koom test his strength on that one."

Others nodded in agreement. For over a year the big log had been locked fast in the sand at the edge of the River Yu as if buried in cement. Even the largest and most powerful of the tuskers, working in pairs and thrusting their tusks deep under the log, had been unable to break it loose from the grip of the hard-packed sand.

Haji's heart beat faster, for this was a challenge he would gladly accept. Leaning over, he whispered to Byoo, "Majda Koom is clever. He knows much about logs in the sand, and he can move this one, too. We will show them."

Byoo flashed his big smile. "It will be good to see," he whispered with complete confidence. "Let me come with you as your paijaik."

"Ket Kay has asked to be paijaik," replied Haji. "But he has no experience as a ground helper. You could come with us as his teacher, and show him what to do with the drag chain and all that needs to be done."

Byoo's smile was bigger than ever as he nodded. "But where is Ket Kay? He has not been at the fires all evening."

"He is losing his fear of the jungle at night," said Haji. He thought no more about it until he returned to their sleeping place in the hut of the wrinkled one and found Ket Kay waiting up for him.

"It is true, what you said about the dacoit with the scar," he whispered. "He did have another reason for coming."

"Why do you say that?"

"I kept watch of his camp by the river. While he sat by his fire a sound came out of the darkness, like the clucking of a jungle hen. The dacoit jumped to his feet. He answered with the same clucking sound. Soon a man came into the light of his fire."

"Did you recognize him?"

"It was one of the tree choppers, the young one, with the light skin."

Haji nodded. The tree chopper was new here, and had come from the Shan Hills only a few weeks ago. "Could you hear what they said?"

"Only a little. Something about brotherhood—the new brotherhood. Have you heard of such?"

"No. But they might be old friends. The dacoit will be gone in the morning. Then you are to be my paijaik. All the oozies are coming to watch while I have Majda Koom dig up a log in the sand."

Having a chance to show off the tremendous strength of his elephant so excited Haji that he hardly slept that night. But in the morning, when Oo Yan heard what was planned, he became angry.

"Let there be no more foolish talk about testing the strength of Majda Koom," he said sharply.

"Please Maung Oo Yan," begged Haji. "Majda Koom can do it."

86

"What he can do or what he cannot do is not the question," answered the chief of the oozies. "He has not worked the logs for over two years. He is not at his full strength. This is not the time to test him on a big log."

Haji hung his head. There was nothing he could say, for Oo Yan was clearly right.

Oo Yan touched him lightly on the shoulder. "It would be well to remember that you have no experience as an oozie. Time is needed for a new oozie and his elephant to work well together."

To give them time to learn to work well together, Oo Yan saw to it that they dragged only the lightest logs and used only the easiest drag paths.

Majda Koom, as well as all the other company elephants, worked for three days, then rested for two. Elephants needed that much rest if they were to be kept in good condition. But even two days of rest would soon not be enough, for the hot dry season was upon them.

Many days had passed since the last rain. In the shade of the deep gorge, where Haji and Majda Koom still went on their resting days, the roar and hiss of plunging water could no longer be heard. Gone, too, were the leaping fish and the flying spray and cooling mists. Even the deep dark pools were drying up.

With each passing day dry winds sent their burning fingers deeper and deeper into the jungle—green things withering, turning yellow, then brown. Drying creepers hardened and broke into brittle wiry stems and flakes that could not tempt even the hungriest elephants.

The big animals began to suffer. Their favorite foods had withered and dried. And now the leafy roof of the jungle, which had sheltered them from the sun as they worked, was beginning to thin out and disappear as dead leaves fell from the trees.

Whenever the elephants were forced to move out of the shade they tried to cover their backs with earth, branches, withered creepers, and anything else that would serve to protect them from the blazing heat of the sun. To them, heat was a serious matter, for elephants cannot sweat. The only sign of their being too hot was a slight dampness around the edges of their large toenails.

At last came the day Haji had been waiting for—the day of the calling in of the elephants, when work in the teak forests came to an end. It was the day Thakin Jensen decided no more work could be done in the awful heat of the dry season without seriously affecting the health of the elephants. They needed a rest and a chance to escape from the scorching heat of the sun. So did the oozies.

That day marked the beginning of a six-week vacation period, and the oozies and their families made ready to leave for their rest camp in the cool evergreen hills far to the north. They loaded all their belongings on the backs of their elephants, also the small children, and even woven cages of cane filled with live chickens and ducks.

The journey took four marches—four full painful days of traveling over parched brown hills where trees stood naked and leafless against the sky, and heat danced

on the rocks, and the rays of the sun beat down merci-
lessly.

Haji walked every step of the way. Majda Koom
followed at his heels, heavily loaded with camp supplies
and sacks of rice and spices. Following close behind
came Ket Kay, gasping for breath and, more often than
not, complaining loudly about the heat.

"Wah! This heat!" he would cry. "I wish the cold
rains would come. I wish the clouds would hide the sun.
Water! If only we can find water in the next stream bed."

Although Haji suffered from the heat as much as
anyone else, Ket Kay's complaints often brought a tight
smile to his lips, for he knew Ket Kay's little secret. Ket
Kay's lagging behind was not caused by weakness due to
heat. No. He lagged so that he could be within easy reach
of Majda Koom's tail. It was a handy thing to grab hold of
and be pulled along by whenever they climbed a steep
hill.

Late one afternoon when they finally arrived at the
rest camp, Ket Kay was still complaining about the heat.
He was among the first to discover the broad flowing
river beside the camp—the mighty Chindwin—and he
was the first to plunge into its soothing waters. Others
followed in a wild and noisy scramble, making for the
river and dashing in to cool their feverish bodies.

In the days that followed—long, lazy, drowsy days
in the deep shade of the evergreens—there was little for
the men and their elephants to do but rest and eat and
sleep, and then rest and eat and sleep again.

At each going down of the sun the elephants would be hobbled and released to feed where they pleased during the night—to search for tender shoots and climbers in the evergreen hills, and for wild plantains on the lower slopes and bottoms, and to eat their fill of the tall grass growing in the swamps and nullahs.

It was there in the swamps and nullahs that they were usually found at dawn by their oozies, who brought them back to camp and to the river to be soaked and rubbed and scrubbed and inspected with loving care. Then, for both men and beasts, followed long sleepy idle hours of rest and napping in the shade.

During those carefree days Haji and Majda Koom never wandered far from camp. They went just far enough to feel they were off by themselves. The great tusker never stood still. If he wasn't rocking slowly from side to side, or flopping his ears, or switching his tail to drive off the flies, or feeling around with the tip of his trunk for a tender green thing to eat, he was picking up a stick to scratch some itch on his back that was too far away to reach with his trunk.

And so it was that the days passed peacefully and pleasantly, one by one, and slowly the elephants and their oozies regained their strength. For Haji, these were happy days. But his feeling of peace suddenly came to an end one evening when Oo Yan came to the campfire with word that the red-faced inspector had at last found an excellent oozie for Majda Koom.

"The new oozie will be waiting for us when

we return to our camp on the River Yu," explained Oo Yan.

Haji stared at the fire and said nothing.

The wrinkled oozie who was sitting nearby rubbed his brown chin thoughtfully as he looked up at Oo Yan. "If this man is an oozie of much excellence, how is it that he has no elephant of his own?" he asked.

"We may learn more of that when he comes to camp," replied Oo Yan. "All we know of him is that his name is Chan Tha."

"Chan Tha?" asked a Karen peddler who was visiting the rest camp. "That one I know. A big man, and strong, from a camp on the Nanpo."

All eyes turned to the Karen peddler. When he did not continue, the wrinkled one shook his head. "Thakin Jensen should have warned the red-faced one against oozies from those northern camps. They are new camps, and they use elephants captured from the wild elephant herds. Such elephannts are trained by treating them cruelly until their spirits are broken."

"Ayee," said another. "They do not understand our way with elephants. They do not know that ours were born in camp and trained with kindness and patience in our elephant school."

Oo Yan turned to the Karen peddler. "What do you know of his elephant?"

"His was a big tusker, and dangerous. He had killed his last oozie before Chan Tha became his rider," answered the Karen. "It is said that Chan Tha has a hard way with elephants, and makes them know who is master."

Haji became so upset he forgot his manners and cried out, "If he is cruel to Majda Koom there will be trouble. I myself will—"

"Enough!" cried Oo Yan. Then he turned once again to the Karen. "What happened to Chan Tha's elephant? Something must have happened to it or he would not be free now to serve as oozie for Majda Koom."

The Karen shook his head. "Of that I have heard nothing. Many days have passed since last I visited at the camp on the Nanpo."

Exactly what had happened to Chan Tha's elephant remained a mystery and was often mentioned by the oozies at evening campfire.

But Haji took little interest in such talk. Nothing mattered to him but the certain knowledge that Majda Koom would soon be taken from him, and there was nothing he could do to prevent it.

Food no longer interested him. At night he tossed and turned for long sleepless hours. The days were easier to bear. They began passing more quickly now, for the time had come to brand the young elephants.

Branding was done with a white paste, stamped on each of the young elephant's hips in the form of a large letter C—the company brand. But the paste had to be washed off again in a few minutes, after being on just long enough to blister the skin but not long enough to eat painfully into the flesh. The blistered skin was then treated daily with soothing oil, and dusted with a powder that kept off the flies until the blisters had healed, leaving a permanent scar in the form of a large letter C.

During their last few days at camp the oozies were kept busy making new harnesses for their elephants. Haji, with the help of Oo Yan and the wrinkled one, tried his hand at making a breast strap for Majda Koom. Using the bark of the bambwe tree, he cut it into strips. These he beat on a rock until they were as soft as the finest leather. He braided the strips together in the form of a wide breast strap that even Majda Koom, with all his strength, would not be able to break on the heaviest log drag.

Then at last, after the first heavy rains of May had turned the world all green and bright and fresh again, they took to the trail on the long journey home.

Once or twice each day Oo Yan came back to walk for a time at Haji's side, as if he sensed the emptiness and the ache in Haji's heart. Sometimes he said nothing. More often he spoke at length of the many good years he and Haji's father had shared together as close friends.

Even on the last day of the journey, with a soft rain splattering down through the leaves, and white mists rising from the bottoms like curtains of swirling smoke, Oo Yan found time to walk for a while at his side.

Later that day, in camp, Oo Yan was again at Haji's side when he finally came face to face with the stranger who was waiting to take Majda Koom from him.

A tall man, Chan Tha walked with a limp as he came

up for a look at Majda Koom. His bushy black brows almost screened his eyes from view—narrow, squinting eyes so deeply set that it was almost impossible to tell which way he was looking. But now he focused his attention on the elephant, completely ignoring Oo Yan, whose white coat clearly marked him out as one in authority to whom respect was due.

Oo Yan spoke out firmly. "This boy is to be your paijaik. In these first days you will find him useful in handling the elephant."

Chan Tha then faced him, clearly annoyed. "Sir, I know what I am about. Never was there an elephant I could not handle, and I have handled many in my time. I need no help from a child."

"Proud words, Chan Tha. I shall hold you to them," said Oo Yan sharply. He turned to Haji. "Come. Your work with this elephant is done. Now the responsibility rests with Chan Tha."

8

An Unseen Witness

No one waited more anxiously for the return of Majda Koom and his new oozie the following morning than did Haji. It was known that Chan Tha had left camp just before dawn to track down and bring back the elephant. But the two did not come in time for the morning bath in the river. They were still missing an hour later when Thakin Jensen held his inspection of the elephants.

Byoo was greatly amused. "Wah!" he said, chuckling. "It may be that the great Chan Tha has been learning a thing or two about elephants from Majda Koom."

Ket Kay laughed and slapped his thigh with delight.

Haji was far too anxious to be amused, for he

remembered what the Karen peddler had said, that Chan Tha had a hard way with elephants. And he remembered Chan Tha's proud boasting, and his quickness to anger.

There was no telling how cruel he might be to an elephant that resisted his will. Haji knew very well that Majda Koom could be stubborn and would continue to resist the man's will unless something was done.

Even before Chan Tha came limping back into camp late that afternoon, saying nothing, Haji had worked out a plan which might sooth the pride of the new oozie and keep him from striking out in anger against Majda Koom.

Up well before dawn the next morning, Haji slipped quietly and unseen into the jungle. For a time he held to the lowlands, skirting some of the highest ridges where Majda Koom usually spent most of the night feeding on jungle greens and shoots of tender bamboo.

There were hills he could not avoid. These he took in swift stride, without so much as a pause to look for tracks of the elephant. That wasn't necessary, for he could hear the singing of Majda Koom's wooden bell long before he reached the lowlands of the nullah. There in the nullah it was Majda Koom's habit to top his night's feeding with a generous breakfast of kaing grass.

Majda Koom came quickly out of the tall grass at his call, as if waiting for him, making the soft chirpings and whistlings of a happy elephant from the first moment he heard Haji's voice.

Tears stung Haji's eyes as he mounted the elephant. But he blinked them away and turned back toward camp.

Somewhere along that trail Chan Tha would be coming for another attempt at capturing the elephant. Haji shuddered at the thought of their meeting. He was afraid and wanted to turn from the trail and flee into the deepest part of the jungle.

Yet he knew he could change nothing by running away. What was to be would be, and there was no way he could change that. All was in the lap of the gods. They had a plan for him, and so far as he could tell their plan was that he should continue along the trail until the moment of meeting.

He had not long to wait. The tall lean limping figure of Chan Tha suddenly appeared before them as they topped a rise in the trail.

Haji stiffened. "I come with your elephant, sir," he cried out in as cheerful a voice as he could manage.

Chan Tha stopped, completely taken by surprise. His lips tightened into a thin hard line, his eyes staring at Haji.

With his heart beating wildly, Haji ordered his elephant to kneel. When it was down, he leaped to the ground and stood waiting politely.

"By whose orders did you come?" demanded Chan Tha.

Haji swallowed and shook his head. "I had no orders, sir. Oo Yan and the thakin know nothing of this."

"You lie!" shouted the man. "Why else would you come?"

"It was the stubbornness of Majda Koom that brought

97

me," Haji explained. "Never has he allowed strangers to approach when he is feeding. But he learns quickly. In a day or two more he will know you as his master."

Chan Tha suddenly reached out and grabbed him firmly by the shoulders. "Do you take me for a fool? Is this a trick, boy? Will they be laughing at the campfires tonight because I needed help to catch my elephant? Is that it, boy?"

"No! No!" cried Haji. "Please, sir, believe me!"

Chan Tha's powerful fingers dug so deeply into his shoulders that he almost cried out in pain. "Who else in camp knows of your coming? Speak up, boy. Answer me!"

"Believe me," begged Haji in a voice that trembled. "No one—not one person in camp knows of this."

For a long moment Chan Tha seemed undecided as he studied him through eyes that were mere slits.

"Hear me well, boy," he said in a voice edged with steel. "See that no one ever learns of this meeting, or you will be made to answer for it."

Haji nodded. "I—I hear," he said, feeling suddenly weak. But he knew that his plan was working. Chan Tha, in spite of his pride and his boasting, was willing to accept secret help during the difficult breaking-in period.

Chan Tha limped over and mounted the elephant. Haji quickly stepped out ahead, leading the way back toward camp, knowing that Majda Koom would follow obediently without resisting his new oozie.

One night several weeks later, Ket Kay moved up behind Haji at the campfire and whispered in his ear: "Go to the elephant bathing place tonight when all is quiet. One will be waiting to speak to you there."

"Who?"

Ket Kay, who seemed to be out of breath, shook his head ever so slightly, and said loudly, "In a little while I will be at the boys' campfire." Then he hurried away.

Haji hardly knew what to think. Without turning his head, he searched the circle of oozies for Chan Tha. As he expected, he did not find him. The man was not well liked by the others, and never joined them at the campfires.

If this was some trick—if Chan Tha had some evil plan to threaten or harm him—but no. That made no sense. If Chan Tha had anything to say to him privately, he would certainly not find it necessary to arrange for a special meeting to say it, since they were alone in the jungle day after day as they worked with Majda Koom on the log drags. And yet?

Haji waited anxiously until he saw Ket Kay return and seat himself at the boys' campfire. He went to join him there.

"What is this whispering?" he asked.

"Ask Oo Yan," replied Ket Kay.

"He gave you the message?"

Ket Kay nodded.

Knowing his secret meeting was to be with Oo Yan

made Haji feel better. Yet it frightened him, too. Oo Yan had not spoken to him for weeks. Why? And now this secret meeting! Had anyone but Ket Kay brought the message, Haji would not have believed it.

He waited until the campfires had faded to glowing red coals and silence had fallen over the camp. Then he slipped quietly into the jungle, not toward the river, but away from it.

Feeling his way in the darkness, he followed a familiar path until it curved and joined a well-worn elephant trail leading to the river. This brought him to the far side of the elephant bathing place where anyone waiting would hardly expect to find him. If it really was Oo Yan, no harm would be done. If it wasn't, he would have time to slip away, if necessary, without being seen.

He paused in the dark fringe of trees and brush lining the edge of the sandy beach. In the dim starlight, he could see no one.

He waited. For a time he heard nothing but the small noises of the night—the singing and buzzing of insects; the occasional splash of a fish, the squawk of a nightjar, the rustling of small creatures in the underbrush.

All at once something on the river drew his attention. The shimmering little threads of starlight dancing along the surface of the water were being broken by the passing of a dark object.

Haji shrank back deeper into the shadows. He stared in amazement. It was a small boat. He could make out two people. Both had paddles, which they were not using as they drifted silently by the elephant camp.

Why were they traveling by night? Now that the heavy rains had come, no one but fools would risk the danger of swift currents and drifting logs in the darkness. Haji almost forgot to breathe as he watched until they had passed out of sight.

Moments later he was startled by the faint sound of footsteps in the sand. He saw a dark figure move out of the shadows. He watched as the man approached. He was not limping.

"Come," said Oo Yan in a strange and guarded voice.

He led the way down the beach, not stopping until they had gone some distance from the elephant camp.

"You saw the boat?" he asked. Then, lowering his voice, he added, "There have been others passing in the night—and comings and goings we know little of. We can only wait and watch—and are being watched."

Haji was frightened. Oo Yan spoke in a voice that did not seem to be his own. "Please, Maung Oo Yan," Haji said. "You speak in riddles."

"There is much we do not know. Today the company sent a warning to all camps. Guns have been stolen. Dacoits are joining bandits from the Shan Hills who call themselves the New Brotherhood. In the last few months three large tuskers from other camps have disappeared, one of these from the camp on the Nanpo. It was Chan Tha's elephant."

Hearing the name Chan Tha sent a chill through Haji. He did not want to think of the man. "If all that disappeared had big tusks, it must be the work of ivory hunters," he said.

"Not so. Ivory hunters kill for the ivory. No dead elephants could be found," answered Oo Yan. "Elephants are now being stolen for another reason, and Majda Koom, the greatest of them all, would be a prize worth taking. He may be in danger."

"Majda Koom could never be taken from us," said Haji. "He would not take orders from oozies he did not know."

"He learned quickly to take orders from Chan Tha," Oo Yan reminded him. "But it was Majda Koom I came to ask you about. A change has come over him. He is restless. Anger builds up in him. Only yesterday he struck out with his trunk at a pye-dog and would have killed him had the blow found its mark."

"All elephants hate pye-dogs," said Haji, trying to defend the elephant.

"Even so, never before has Majda Koom struck out at one. What has happened to him? How is it that we find cuts and scratches on his head and ears at every inspection?"

Haji kept his lips tightly sealed. Chan Tha seemed to enjoy making the animal suffer, often beating him over the head with the ankus, his elephant stick. He had even sharpened the steel points of the ankus so that he could stab and hook at the big ears at the slightest excuse. But of all this Haji dared not say a word.

Oo Yan said, "Chan Tha is new here and how far he can be trusted we do not know. You have nothing to fear from him. He will never know of our secret meeting here. I have even avoided you in camp these past few weeks so that he would have no reason to suspect you were carrying tales of him. You can speak freely."

Haji hung his head and remained silent.

"Sometimes silence speaks plainer than words, little brother," said Oo Yan gently. "But you may find your tongue quickly enough when I tell you that today Chan Tha came asking for another paijaik. You make trouble, he says, and he no longer wants you as ground helper. What do you say to that?"

Haji's throat went dry. If he were to lose his job as ground helper, he would be losing Majda Koom as well, for they would no longer be spending their days together on the log drags.

"Do not listen to him, Maung Oo Yan," he begged. "It is not true that I make trouble. Majda Koom, as everyone knows, is always more gentle when I am near."

"Yes. That may be the very heart of the problem," said Oo Yan thoughtfully. "Chan Tha has been told that you will continue as his paijaik. But remember this: he is a man of pride. Take care not to offend, or to let the love you and Majda Koom have for each other shine through too plainly."

Haji felt a sting of guilt. He had never missed a chance to pat Majda Koom affectionately on the trunk. It had pleased him that the elephant was always looking about to see where he was. It had given him a feeling of pride whenever the tip of the elephant's trunk slipped into his hand as they walked side by side. Most of all it had given him a warm happy feeling to have Majda Koom show his love by coming to stand over him as he rested during the noon hour.

Haji now realized he had let his love shine through too plainly. He had encouraged the little attentions Majda Koom had always given him, even though he knew that they angered Chan Tha.

No longer could he afford to annoy Chan Tha in any way—not if he wished to continue as Chan Tha's paijaik. And so it happened, in the days that followed, that he took great care to keep a distance between himself and Majda Koom.

He walked no more at the elephant's side, no longer gave him a friendly pat on the trunk, and even put an end to the happy, carefree hours they usually spent together in the jungle on the elephant resting days.

Then, one morning, a week later, Chan Tha went to test the elephant's strength on the huge sand-locked log that lay buried near the black rocks by the River Yu. At Chan Tha's direction, Majda Koom thrust his great tusks into the hard-packed sand under one end of the log and strained with all his might.

"Lift! Lift!" yelled Chan Tha, becoming impatient.

Majda Koom forced his tusks even deeper into the sand and tried again. The log did not budge.

"The other end!" shouted Chan Tha.

Withdrawing his tusks, Majda Koom moved to the other end of the log, dug in again, and slowly gathered his tremendous strength to force the log up out of the sand.

"Hmah! Hmah!" yelled Chan Tha angrily. "Lift, lift, you fool!"

Majda Koom did his best. He strained and grunted and heaved and lifted until his muscles quivered from the effort. But the log might as well have been embedded in solid cement. It did not move.

"Lift! Lift!" screamed Chan Tha, losing his temper. He began clubbing the elephant over the head with his ankus. Majda Koom squealed with pain.

The squeal shot through Haji like a stab of cold steel. Never before had he heard Majda Koom cry out in pain, and it frightened him. How much more would the elephant take?

"No!" cried Haji. "Maung Chan Tha, listen! Please! That is not the way my father did it. Do not hurry him!"

Chan Tha let out a string of curses. "I am oozie here!" he roared.

The unwanted advice only made him angrier than ever. Again and again he forced the elephant to dig his tusks under the log and strain and heave. Each new failure brought on another burst of temper, and made Chan Tha more determined than ever.

The elephant finally reached the point where he could do no more. Ignoring the screams and blows of his oozie, he backed off to catch his breath.

Chan Tha, beside himself with rage, screamed and cursed like a man gone mad. He began a savage attack, slashing and stabbing with the sharp steel points of his ankus until the big ears ran with blood.

Suddenly Majda Koom could take no more. He jerked up his head and trumpeted an angry warning. Up swung the great trunk. Haji saw it coil for a deadly blow and he knew what was coming.

"No! Majda! Stop!" he screamed.

It was too late. He watched in horror as the mighty trunk lashed back at the oozie on his neck.

Chan Tha ducked. He took a glancing blow on his hand. The ankus went flying as he slipped and fell to the ground.

Haji dashed between them before the elephant could strike again. For an instant Majda Koom, still trumpeting and snorting with rage, threatened to push him aside to get at the fallen oozie.

"No! No! Big brother, no!" cried Haji.

He caught the trunk in his arms and held on and began speaking to the elephant in the low, calm voice Majda Koom knew so well. He finally managed to back him off to a safe distance and held him there till he quieted.

Slowly Chan Tha picked himself up from the ground, and brushed the dust from his side. He glared at Haji.

"You will pay for this, both of you," he said slowly and in a voice so quiet, so edged with deadly purpose, that it made Haji's skin crawl.

Exactly what Chan Tha meant by his threat Haji found out later that day in camp when Oo Yan came looking for him.

"Your service as paijaik is finished," he said, looking bitterly disappointed. "Ket Kay is to take your place with Chan Tha. You will report for work at the elephant school in the morning."

Haji felt nothing. He had expected the worst, and now that he had lost Majda Koom, he was too empty, too dead inside to care where they asked him to work.

Oo Yan scowled. "Chan Tha told us you ordered the elephant to strike at him. And he brought with him a witness to prove it."

"A witness?" Haji asked weakly. "I—I saw no one there but Chan Tha."

"The thakin and I have seen Majda Koom's ears. We are convinced that Chan Tha and his witness lied. But when the inspector comes in a few days again we know he will surely take the word of Chan Tha and his witness against anything you or we can say." He shook his head sadly. "No good can come out of this. That we know."

9

At the Elephant School

The day soon came when all was ready at the elephant school. A training pen, in the shape of a narrow triangle, had been built of logs in the center of the clearing. It was just large enough to hold one five-year-old elephant. The logs had been stripped of bark and rubbed smooth. Haji and Byoo had spent hours greasing them with the fat of a roasted pig to prevent the young elephants from injuring themselves in their struggles to escape.

Near the head of the training pen the oozies had constructed a small wooden shrine, no larger than a Burmese dollhouse, which they whitewashed and covered with a thatched roof of rice straw from the valley. Into this shrine, before the early morning fog had lifted from the river, women and children placed cups of cooked rice, a dish of water, a boiled egg, and a large red frangipani blossom as offerings to win the favor of the nats, the evil spirits of the jungle.

As usual, it had rained most of the night. The heavy fragrance of jungle flowers and damp earth still hung in the cool morning air when the oozies and their families, dressed in their best and brightest silks, came for the opening ceremony. Oo Yan was among them, easy to spot in his crisp white coat.

The children and pye-dogs soon became restless and began running about. So did the young elephants who were about to be trained. But the nine mother elephants and their oozies waited quietly in line at one end of the clearing. In front of them stood the koonkie, the school-master elephant. He was big and gentle, known for his patience, and had served as koonkie for many years.

No one could have been happier or more excited than Byoo. "Today is the day I become a real oozie and have an elephant of my very own," he told Haji, wearing his brightest smile. "I have waited for this day all my life!"

Haji smiled and nodded. He and Byoo had grown up together in the elephant camp, had become paijaiks together on the same day, and had dreamed of becoming oozies together, each with his own young elephant to train at the elephant school.

"Please, Haji, it is not too late," begged Byoo. "Choose a calf for yourself. Become an oozie with me.

Why do you wait and wait and wait when you know that Majda Koom . . . Haji, you do not listen!"

"Chan Tha burns with hate for Majda Koom. Never will he forget that Majda Koom struck at him. It is in my head that some bad thing soon will happen."

"Awah!" exclaimed Byoo impatiently. "What greater harm could he do that he . . ." Suddenly forgetting what he was about to say, Byoo leaned closer and whispered, "Look! She is coming!"

The girl, smiling shyly as she came up, was dressed in silks of brightest blue. Her fresh young face was the color of wild honey. Her black hair, brushed back from her face, was glossy with coconut oil. Above one ear she wore a white trumpet blossom, still fresh with morning dew.

"By your leave I bring this offering to the shrine," she said timidly, holding out a small cup of boiled rice. "It—it is for luck to you and your elephant, Byoo."

"Wah!" Byoo grinned broadly. It took him a moment to find his tongue. "That—that big calf over there is mine. It is the one that liked to chase people. I call her Taw Sin Ma."

"Taw Sin Ma," she said, smiling shyly. "It is a good name."

They watched as she walked swiftly away to place her offering of rice in the shrine for the nats.

"She is the one I told you about," whispered Byoo. He giggled. "Whenever we meet she is always giving to me the sweet smile. Is she not pretty?"

Before Haji could answer, a sudden stir of excitement drew his attention. The wrinkled one had come into the clearing with the white candles of the ceremony. His timing was perfect, for the first rays of the morning sun were just touching the swaying tops of the royal palms.

With great care he arranged the candles in a circle about the nat shrine. There were sixteen of them, one for each year of training and living it would take before the young elephants became fully grown and strong enough to be of use on the log drags. By then they would be twenty-one years of age.

A hush fell over the crowd as the wrinkled one lighted the candles. They burned down quickly. When the last one finally flickered and went out a cheer went up from the crowd. The mischievous nats had been given their dues, the ceremony was over, and the work of training could begin.

"Your calf will be first, Byoo," said the wrinkled one. "Bring it up to the pen."

With balls of cooked rice and tamarind fruit Byoo tempted the calf closer and closer to the pen, until she stood at the opening. But there she became suspicious and would not enter.

Quietly the koonkie, the big schoolmaster elephant, was brought up behind her. Haji, who had taken a position inside the pen, came forward a few steps and offered her a banana.

She reached in as far as she could, snatched it from his hand and gobbled it with relish. He backed a step,

111

offered her another. Moving in, she took it eagerly, for these were not the ordinary tasteless little wild bananas, but big delicious yellow-ripe ones brought in by bullock cart from the Valley of Ten Villages.

Backing away, Haji held out a whole bunch of bananas. She made a grab for them. But Haji leaped back just in time. He pretended to be so frightened by her lunge that he dropped the bananas and slipped between the logs to safety outside the pen.

The temptation was too much for Taw Sin Ma. She dashed deep into the pen to pick up the bananas. At the same instant the koonkie moved up behind her and pushed against her rear to prevent her from backing out. He held her there until two heavy bars had been slipped into place behind her.

Taw Sin Ma found herself in a cage for the first time in her life. Kicking and squealing, she struggled desperately to get out. When she stopped to rest, Haji tried to calm her by offering her a banana between the bars.

Refusing it, she began fighting her cage again, rolling and kicking and lunging against the well-greased logs. One burst of temper followed another. Almost an hour passed before she finally gave up in disgust and accepted the fruit Haji offered her.

"She is ready!" he shouted, looking up at Byoo, who sat in a kind of swing formed by a loop of rope. It hung from a strong branch directly over the training pen.

Byoo checked the pulley above his head to see that the rope was not jammed. Then he signaled to the oozies

at the pulling end of the rope and they lowered him slowly until he sat on the neck of the calf.

Taw Sin Ma exploded with rage, but not before Byoo had been hauled up, well out of danger. She soon quieted enough to be bribed with another banana. Down came Byoo again and sat on her neck, and up he went an instant later as she burst into another fit of rage.

Byoo was lowered to her neck again and again. The struggle continued all through the morning, seemingly without end. But by noon little Taw Sin Ma was so very tired that she allowed Byoo to sit on her neck for as long as half an hour at a time.

Byoo laughed. "She is learning!"

"She may be resting," said the wrinkled one. "Do not let her rest. Bring down the weight."

A heavy, well-padded block of wood, suspended from the branch on another pulley, was lowered until it rested lightly on the elephant's back. This brought on more bucking and kicking. The block was lifted, but came down again as soon as the calf quieted.

The struggle continued for an hour or so, with Taw Sin Ma never being given a moment's rest. She finally reached the limit of her strength, and her legs gave way under the weight of the heavy block. As she sank slowly to the ground the oozies yelled, "Hmit! Hmit! Hmit! Get down! Get down! Get down!"

The large block of wood was lifted after it had held her down to the ground for several minutes. "Tah! Tah! Tah! Get up! Get up! Get up!" chanted the oozies in chorus, and they kept up the chanting until she rose to her feet. In this way the weight was used over and over again to teach her that "Hmit!" was the command for down and "Tah!" was the command for up.

The training continued throughout the long hours of the afternoon, with Haji always ready to pet and talk to her gently and to offer her bananas and short lengths of juicy sugar cane at every pause.

Slowly Taw Sin Ma learned her first great lesson—that man was her master, and that she had no choice but to obey, for he would never give up until she had done what was asked of her.

The wrinkled one, chief trainer of the elephant school, had unending patience and was not easily pleased. The sun had already set beyond the dark rim of trees on the other side of the river before he was finally satisfied that Taw Sin Ma had learned her lesson well. By then the little calf was so well trained that she went down whenever Byoo pressed down on her back with his hand and said, "Hmit!"

The following morning Taw Sin Ma was tied to a nearby tree by one of her hind legs. Byoo now had to continue her training alone. He ordered her down and he ordered her up time after time, and once in a while he sat on her neck for an hour or more.

Meanwhile, another calf had been brought into the training pen. There Haji, as one of the wrinkled one's assistants, was again offering bribes of fruit and sugar cane as he had done the day before.

The work of training had continued for several hours when Haji heard someone shout his name. He turned to see Ket Kay come running. He looked frightened.

"Come!" he gasped. "Quick! Oo Yan asks for you!"

He turned before Haji could question him and ran back the way he had come. Leaping to his feet, Haji followed, his heart hammering. Oo Yan would have only one reason for wanting him to come, and that was to help with Majda Koom.

"What happened?" he asked, as they entered the jungle. "What of Majda Koom?"

"Oo Yan will let no one go near him," answered Ket Kay. "He makes the big angry noises."

"But what of Chan Tha? Where is he?"

"Majda Koom struck him down," replied Ket Kay. "He does not move."

Long before they reached the towpath, they could hear the angry trumpeting and snorting of Majda Koom. Haji did not have to be told why he was angry. Chan Tha had been punishing him cruelly again with the sharp points of his ankus.

As they approached, Oo Yan hurried to meet them. "See what you can do with Majda Koom," he said. "He is not far away from where Chan Tha lies on the towpath. But the elephant becomes excited whenever any of us try to go near."

Haji nodded. He stepped out onto the towpath where he could be seen by Majda Koom. "I come! It is I, Haji, who comes for you, big brother," he called. "I come! I come! I come!"

Walking slowly forward, still calling out to the elephant, he soon came abreast of the fallen oozie.

Chan Tha watched without moving a muscle. The man did not seem to be badly hurt, but he knew enough about angry elephants to lie perfectly still. Even the slightest move might excite the elephant and cause him to attack again.

Haji continued his slow advance. He began talking softly now, soothingly, with love in his voice, for he knew there was nothing to fear. Majda Koom had stopped trumpeting. He had spread out his ears and was listening and watching as Haji came closer.

Now, as every good oozie knows, an angry elephant should never be approached without first ordering him to the ground. This is a simple test of obedience. If the elephant obeyed the command, he was under control and could be approached without danger. But if he failed to go down, he was not under control, and the oozie would know better than to go within reach of his powerful trunk.

Haji knew all this, but he also knew Majda Koom. The elephant had been a trusted and well-loved member of his family for as long as he could remember, and he walked up to him boldly and with complete confidence.

Not until he gave the elephant an affectionate pat did he notice the twitching and trembling of his trunk and the strange look in his eyes, a wild look Haji had never seen before. He knew he had to act quickly to get the elephant well away from the fallen oozie.

"Come, big brother," he said softly, and started

walking past him along the towpath. Majda Koom turned and followed.

When they were out of sight around a bend Haji raised his arms. The elephant lifted him to his neck. An instant later, Majda Koom bolted, rushing headlong into the jungle in a wild burst of speed.

Haji caught hold of the big ears and hung on. There was nothing more he could do until Majda Koom's furious rage had burned itself out. The elephant finally slowed down to a walk. Even then Haji allowed him to wander about aimlessly for a time before heading him back to camp.

Haji was called to the thakin's house later that afternoon. There he was told to serve as oozie for several days while Chan Tha recovered from his injuries.

The thakin took the pipe out of his mouth and smiled. "It may surprise you to know that Chan Tha himself suggested that you serve as oozie till he is well again. He is convinced that you saved his life today. But I must warn you that the inspector will be coming again in three or four days and his inspection of the elephants will not be an easy one."

Haji was not worried. The inspector's visit had been put off several times already because of the danger of roving bands of outlaws.

"This time he will not be delayed," added the thakin. "This time the government is sending an armed guard of soldiers to protect him."

The inspection would include an examination of

elephant harnesses also. But neither Haji nor Ket Kay could find Majda Koom's new harness on the harness racks.

Since the old one could be used just as well on the towpaths, Haji thought no more about it till he met Ket Kay at the harness racks two mornings later. Ket Kay, serving as his paijaik, had the new harness in his arms, but he looked troubled.

"Something is wrong, Haji," he said, shaking his head and blinking his big eyes. "Last night, when I went to ask Chan Tha about the new harness, I saw him walking as well as ever he did. He lied to the thakin about hurting his leg. There is nothing wrong with it. He could work. Why would he have you work in his place?"

Haji frowned. "He told the thakin I saved his life. This may be his way of rewarding me."

"No, no, do not trust him, Haji. It is in my head that he is planning to make trouble for you. Last night when I went to his camp he had a visitor—the same young tree chopper I saw talking to the dacoit who came as messenger that time."

"Wah! That one is always friendly. He talks to everyone."

"This was no friendly talk," protested Ket Kay. "They did not see me, and I watched. Chan Tha was excited. He was explaining something, talking fast, using his hands, pointing to the hills. Then the tree chopper nodded his head and hurried away like one going on important business."

119

"What important business could a tree chopper have?" asked Haji, smiling faintly as he tried to calm his friend.

"You can smile," said Ket Kay, greatly annoyed. "But Oo Yan should hear of this!"

"Go then. And when you have told him, you will find me by the black rocks."

Ket Kay looked surprised. "Where the big log lies in the sand?"

Haji nodded. "If the red-faced one comes today, he will take Majda Koom from me again. I have only this day left to prove that Majda Koom can move the log."

On his way to the black rocks with Majda Koom, Haji passed quite close to the camp of Chan Tha near the river. He wondered again why Chan Tha should want to camp alone at some distance from the other oozies.

Ket Kay caught up with him just as they reached the black rocks and the log that was locked in the sand.

"Oo Yan did not smile when I told him," said Ket Kay breathlessly. "And, Haji, do you know who Chan Tha brought to the thakin's house that day as a witness against you? It was the same young tree chopper. Oo Yan told me just now!"

"But the tree chopper was not there!" said Haji. He could not imagine why the young man would want to lie for Chan Tha.

Taking a deep breath he turned his attention to the big log. He had Majda Koom dig under it with his tusks and lift. They worked for a while on one end, then the other.

"Try the other side of the log," said Haji.

The elephant did. He pushed and lifted and heaved and strained with all his might, but the log did not move an inch.

"You can do it, big brother. You can do it," Haji said softly over and over again. But he knew enough not to hurry the elephant.

Majda Koom finally backed off and stood for a time flopping his ears and switching at flies with his tail.

Ket Kay shook his head. "Even Majda Koom is not strong enough to do it," he said, keenly disappointed.

"Wait! Give him time!" Said Haji. "Majda Koom has always been good at digging logs out of sand. And my father never hurried him."

After resting a bit, Majda Koom walked up to the log again, looked it over carefully, walked around it as if to study it from all sides.

Then he moved up and put one foot on it, pressing down gingerly. Finding the log firm, he stepped up and walked on it from one end to the other and turning, walked back to the place where he had started.

Haji suddenly laughed. "I know! I know!" he yelled to Ket Kay. "I remember now. Watch him!"

Majda Koom stepped off the log. Haji slid down the face of the elephant, caught hold of a tusk and dropped to the ground.

Placing his front feet on one end of the log, Majda Koom pressed down on it several times, then suddenly reared high on his hind legs and slammed down on it with all the force of his tremendous weight.

"Again," said Haji.

Majda Koom struck down once more with his front legs, and did it once again.

"Now the other end," ordered Haji.

The big tusker followed him to the other end, and again he reared and struck down, driving the log deeper into the sand.

"I see it! The sand has let go!" screamed Ket Kay, jumping up and down with excitement.

"My father once told me how he and Majda Koom used to do this," explained Haji. "Sometimes the big weight of Majda Koom is even stronger than the force of his strength!"

Now Majda Koom needed no orders. The great beast thrust his powerful tusks deep into the sand at one end of the log. Then gathering himself, heaving and straining with mighty effort, he slowly forced the end of the log up out of its bed of sand.

Haji laughed with pride. Ket Kay cheered, and came running with the heavy chain with which the log could be dragged into the water.

When that was done, they went inland to the log Oo Yan had ordered them to do that day. But to reach the towpath with it, Majda Koom first had to clear a way through a stand of young trees. This he did with his powerful trunk, ripping up trees by their roots and casting them aside as if they were so many tall reeds.

Too late, Haji saw that his elephant had uprooted a tree in which weaver birds had their nest. He stiffened and leaned back—his signal for the elephant to stop.

"Easy, big brother," he said. "That tree is the home of the weaver birds. Hold it straight up. Careful now! Stand it against that big tree."

Carefully Majda Koom leaned the young tree against the larger one. The nest was undamaged, Haji saw with relief, but the weaver birds were greatly excited.

"Have no fear, little friends," cried Haji. "Your babies are safe and no one will harm them."

But long after that, even after they had reached the towpath and Majda Koom had dragged the log for some distance, Haji could not get the weaver birds out of his mind. It was clearly not the will of the gods that the weavers should have their home disturbed. Yet the accident had happened. Haji wondered if it was a warning of something evil to come.

The evil came sooner than he had expected. Just as they reached the stream where the log was to be left, a scream shattered the jungle stillness.

10

The New Brotherhood Strikes

Angry shouts were coming from upstream. Haji turned in time to see two men struggling with each other on the neck of an elephant. One slipped. He dragged the other with him as he fell to the ground.

Haji watched in amazement. Though he had lived in the elephant camp most of his life, he had never seen anything like this before.

He was able to recognize one of the men as Theebaw, an oozie from camp. Theebaw seemed to be stunned by the fall. He was struggling to get up when the other, a stranger, rushed at him with a rock in his hand.

Theebaw's elephant wheeled at the same instant. It

caught up the stranger in its trunk and, for a moment, held the struggling man high about its head.

The stranger screamed as the elephant threw him. Then he was flying through the air, turning head over heels. He landed with a splash in the middle of the stream. But he was up again in a moment. He thrashed and splashed his way through knee-deep water to the far shore and quickly disappeared from view in the jungle.

Haji was the first to reach Theebaw. "What happened?" he asked. "Who was that?"

"That one! He asked too many questions about the elephants," grumbled Theebaw, bathing his scratched arm in the water. "Wah! He would not even believe when I told him the elephants were let loose each night to feed in the jungle."

"Why was he up on the elephant with you?" asked Haji.

Theebaw scowled. "Back in the jungle he offered me a rupee to let him ride with me to the river. When we reached here and dropped the log, he tried to push me off the elephant. It was a trick to steal Bo Gyi from me."

Other oozies came running, asking questions, talking loudly to each other. "Never before have I heard of a bandit trying to steal an elephant," said one.

"This was no ordinary dacoit," said another. "He must be one of the New Brotherhood. I have heard it said they mean to form an army strong enough to take over the country."

"Ayee," said another. "It is well that the red-faced inspector comes with soldiers."

Majda Koom gave a loud snort of impatience that made Haji hurry back to him. They were done for the day, and the elephant was hot and tired and eager for his bath.

"I will follow in a little while," said Ket Kay, who clearly wanted to stay and listen to the talk of the oozies.

Haji mounted his elephant, and turned to follow the trail to the road of the bullock carts.

The sun was still high when Haji and his huge tusker reached the road. Turning left, he headed down the road toward their usual afternoon bathing place at the bend of the River Yu. There the water ran deep, and the bottom was hard sand. Majda Koom had bathed there every afternoon when work was done and, being a creature of habit, would not have enjoyed bathing anywhere else.

As they followed the road, Haji's brown body swayed loosely with the ambling gait of his elephant. His good humor came bubbling up as he looked fondly down at the great curved tusks of his elephant. In all Burma there was not another pair of tusks half so magnificent. But the tusks were stained and gritty now with the day's work.

"Wah!" laughed Haji. "But for my polishing, big brother, you would soon grow moss on those handsome tusks of yours."

As they rounded a bend in the road a bullock cart came into view. It stood in the middle of the road, and was heavily loaded. But there were no bullocks about,

128

and no sign of the driver. A very strange place to leave a loaded bullock cart, Haji thought, and he studied it with growing suspicion.

Perhaps the bandits had struck and ran off with the bullocks. Many strange things were happening in the hills these days. But as Haji came closer, he saw no reason for concern. What was there for him to fear when he sat on the neck of the mighty Majda Koom? Even the royal tiger and the water buffalo ran away from him. And he was not interested in bandits of the New Brotherhood. All such matters, he believed, should be left in the hands of the gods.

He was almost up to the bullock cart when the elephant suddenly shied. Foliage rustled at the sides of the road. Prickles of fear shot up Haji's back as his eyes caught the metallic glint of guns.

A dozen or more bandits stepped silently into the road. They were grim, and their eyes looked black with hate.

A wild-eyed Karen threw up his rifle. "No tricks," he warned.

After the first terrible instant, Haji steadied his elephant. His greatest fear was that the animal might suddenly bolt and draw their fire. At so close a range, and with a target as big as an elephant, the guns could not miss.

Stroking Majda Koom's massive head he watched the approaching bandits. They were a strangely mixed lot: rice farmers from the valley, filthy dacoits in loincloths, the tall Karen with burning eyes, a light-skinned youth who probably came from the Shan Hills, and two Chinese.

One of the Chinese in a tattered brown uniform waved to the others to halt. Then to Haji he gave a curt command, "Get down!"

With a feeling of helplessness, Haji ordered his elephant down. "One cannot fight the storm, or push back the wind," his wise father had often said. "All things are in the laps of the gods."

Haji managed a quick glance back up the road, but Ket Kay was not in sight. As he dismounted and faced the Chinese leader he wondered if this, too, was the will of the gods.

"You have been greatly honored," said the Chinese leader, watching him closely. "You and your splendid elephant have been selected to serve in the great cause of the New Brotherhood. By authority of General Pen Kin Dot of the People's Army of Liberation, I now accept you into our service."

Haji swallowed. These were strange people—speaking of honor and threatening him with their guns at the same time. He could not believe what was happening to him. And yet, he was pleased to know that they recognized a good elephant when they saw one. That, at least, was in their favor.

Haji offered a timid nod and said, "You could not find a better elephant anywhere in the upper valley of the Irrawaddy."

The tall Karen with the wild eyes edged closer. "I do not trust this nurser of elephants," he said.

"Nor I," snapped the leader. "Keep him under your guns at all times until we reach the General. These supplies must get through without delay. Now get that elephant loaded.

Loading an elephant was no simple matter. The bandits had only a few short ropes made from bark. They also tried to use Majda Koom's light hobble chain. But it soon became clear that the bandits knew nothing about loading an elephant. Haji watched their awkward fumbling in amazement, and sometimes almost felt like laughing out loud.

But whenever he had a chance, he glanced up the road for some sign of Ket Kay. Had Ket Kay followed him? Had he seen what was happening? Was he now running back to camp for help?

All his hopes suddenly died when Ket Kay, with the light-skinned youth beside him and two dacoits with rifles following behind him, came marching down the dusty road of the bullock carts.

The light-skinned youth, a boy of not more than sixteen, grinned broadly as he came up to Haji. "Were you not expecting Ket Kay to follow?" he asked.

"I told him nothing!" yelled Ket Kay.

"Nor did he tell me your name is Haji," the light-skinned one said. He laughed, enjoying himself immensely. "Look at me. Do I not look like someone you both have seen before?"

Haji studied him. The boy's light skin, the way he walked and held his head, even the face itself seemed strangely familiar. And suddenly Haji knew.

"You look like the young tree chopper in camp from the Shan Hills," he said.

"We are brothers," said the boy, laughing. "Without his help and the help of Chan Tha, we would never have been able to set this trap for you."

Haji and Ket Kay exchanged glances. Haji licked his dry lips. He felt sick. "But—but why did Chan Tha help? He could have brought the elephant to you himself."

"Men like Chan Tha and my brother are needed in the elephant camps to send us information and send us elephants. Chan Tha sent us another good elephant only a few months ago."

"Enough talk," growled the Karen.

"What is the danger?" asked the light-skinned boy. "These two are not fools. They cannot run faster than our bullets."

By this time it had become clear that help was needed in loading the elephant. Haji was ordered to build a holder for the cargo.

With Ket Kay helping him, he showed them how to split bamboo and weave it into a large basketlike platform, or pannier, which would fit over the elephant's back. Everyone helped, working swiftly, and within an hour a pannier of sorts was completed. After securing it to Majda Koom's back, it was loaded with the bags of rice, boxes, and guns that came from the bullock cart.

Haji noticed that the leader and the tall Karen were taking a keen interest in his elephant. That cheered him a little, for it seemed like a good sign. He could always get along well with people who liked elephants.

When everything had been loaded, they started off through pathless jungle, being guided by a high peak far in the distance. Haji and Ket Kay were forced to walk just in front of the elephant, with the ever watchful Karen and three guards following close behind. The light-skinned boy and several others went on ahead to hunt and set up camp.

Presently one of the guards came up to walk at Haji's side. "Never have I seen so large an elephant," he said, trying to make friendly conversation.

Haji said nothing.

A few minutes later the guard tried again. "It is well you came down the road when you did," he said. "Never again will you have to be a slave in an elephant camp. Now you are free. Now you are one of the New Brotherhood."

Haji looked at the guard's gun.

The guard caught his meaning. "The gun is only necessary for a little time," he explained. "When you hear all the wonderful things the General has to say about the New Brotherhood, you will no longer want to escape. You believe in brotherhood, do you not?"

"It may be good to have brothers," answered Haji cautiously.

Ket Kay said, "There are good brothers and bad brothers. In my village there are brothers who do not like each other."

"You do not understand the meaning of true brotherhood. That is because you slaves in the elephant camps are kept ignorant by your masters," explained the guard.

133

"They do not want you to hear of the New Brotherhood. They fear it."

"So do I," said Ket Kay.

"There is no need to fear," said the guard. "If you listen, I will tell you why: when the New Brotherhood comes into power, all men will be equal. Can you understand what that will mean? None will be rich. None will be poor. None will go hungry. All will have plenty. All will be free. And best of all, no one will be your master. Would it not be good to live in a world like that where all men are brothers?"

"Wah!" exclaimed Haji. "Such a world—why, it would be almost like living among the gods. But how can we have such a world? When will it happen?"

In his eagerness to learn more, he asked many questions. The answers filled his mind with glowing pictures of a world more wonderful than any he had ever imagined.

Much as he hated to leave his friends in the elephant camp, Haji was almost glad now that he had been captured. Some day he would come back to them and they would all be happy and equal and good brothers together. Even his crippled father would no longer be poor, and his family would always have plenty.

How happy he and Majda Koom could be without masters to tell them what to do, and without red-faced inspectors to trouble them. Nor would they ever have to work again unless they felt like it, and they would always be free to go and come, and always have plenty.

134

11

The Will of the Gods

For a time they walked in silence, Haji taking long easy strides, for he had lost most of his fear. Now he was looking forward to meeting the General who could tell him all about the wonderful New Brotherhood.

Ket Kay looked unhappy and frightened. He edged closer to whisper, "Do not trust them, Haji."

"Wait," said Haji. "Wait till we hear what the General has to say."

"It is in my head that the General is a liar, too," answered Ket Kay. "How can dacoits make good brothers?"

"What is he saying?" asked the guard.

"He wonders how dacoits can be good brothers," said Haji. "It is a sensible question."

The guard laughed. "When all are equal there will be no need for stealing from others. And if there is no stealing, there will be no dacoits."

Haji frowned thoughtfully. He could not quite understand why there would be no stealing when all were equal. It seemed to him that there would always be people who would want to be more than equal, and have more than others.

They came presently to a clear mountain brook and paused to drink and rest a little. The water reminded Haji that Majda Koom had not had his afternoon bath. The least he could do, Haji decided, was to take a moment to wash the sand and grime off the great curved tusks.

When he had finished washing them he turned to the Karen and said modestly, "Are they not splendid tusks?"

The Karen let out a string of curses. "Do you think we have no eye to see? At the end of this journey, you nurser of elephants, it will be for you to cut those fine tusks from the elephant's head."

Haji could hardly believe his ears. "Cut off the tusks of Majda Koom? That cannot be! Without tusks he could not dig up logs in the teakwood forests."

"The New Brotherhood will not use him to dig up logs in the forests," snapped the Karen. "The General himself will order you to cut off his tusks. Ivory brings a good price, and the tusks can be traded for supplies to serve the cause of the New Brotherhood."

To serve the cause! Haji sucked in his breath as the horrible truth suddenly struck him like a club. These

136

men were barbarians! They were savages of the lowest sort. Haji knew in his heart that the gods would never want Majda Koom's glorious tusks to be cut down to ugly stumps.

What could such men as these know about brotherhood? They could not even act as brothers among themselves. Of this Haji felt certain, for life in the elephant camp had taught him that those who were cruel to animals were also cruel to each other.

He wanted no part of their fake brotherhood. Somehow, he knew, he would have to find a way to escape with his elephant.

Darkness had already fallen when they finally reached camp in a thick stand of ironwood trees. The cool night air was laden with the smells of wood smoke and roasting meat, for the carcass of a sambur deer was being turned on a spit over a fire. Fat sputtered in the licking flames.

"Hmit! Hmit!" said Haji, ordering his elephant down some distance from the fire.

The Chinese leader cursed and came running over. "What are you doing?" he demanded.

"I have ordered my elephant down so that we can unload him," answered Haji politely.

"Unload!" screamed the leader. "Who gave orders to unload? Who?"

"Is this not the place where we stop for the night?" asked Haji.

"There will be no unloading this night," snapped

the leader. "We would lose an hour if we had to stop to load again in the morning."

"But—"

"Silence! Get your elephant up again!"

Hot anger suddenly burned in Haji's cheeks. This man was mad. He expected a tired elephant to stand fully loaded all through the night. In a fit of rage, Haji sprang to the elephant's side, jerked loose the belly rope and, with a mighty heave, dumped the platform and the cargo onto the ground. "Tah! Get up!" he commanded Majda Koom.

Screaming curses, the Chinese leader suddenly came to life. He rushed at Haji and struck him in the face. Haji went sprawling to the ground.

"I will teach you obedience!" he roared. "Get him! Hang him in a tree!"

As the guards closed in, Majda Koom wheeled to face them and trumpeted menacingly. The guards stopped in their tracks, suddenly uncertain of themselves.

Haji rose slowly to his feet. "It is well none of you tried to lay hands on me."

The leader's face went purple with rage. The man seemed to be choking.

But the Karen came forward with a crafty smile. "There is a better way to teach obedience," he said quietly. "This nurser of elephants has boasted about how well his elephant digs out logs with his tusks. We have saws in those boxes. We will have him cut off those tusks tonight."

138

The leader looked confused. "What have tusks to do with obedience?"

"Without tusks the animal cannot dig logs," explained the Karen. "This nurser of elephants takes great pride in those tusks. He would be ashamed to bring a tuskless animal back to the logging camp."

The leader's face brightened with understanding. "And so he would not want to go back to the logging camp and would no longer think of escape, or of resisting our commands. Yes, that is true. Find the saws and bring them here. The tusks shall be cut off tonight."

For Haji the words were like a sentence of death. As he saw men rush to the cargo boxes scattered on the ground to search for the saws, his heart began hammering like a wild thing within him.

The Karen was right. If Majda Koom's tusks were cut, Haji knew he could never go back to the elephant camp to face Thakin Jensen and Oo Yan, nor would he ever dare face his crippled father again in the village of Chinwa.

He glanced about at the jungle darkness and, for a moment, was tempted to make a run for it, knowing that Majda Koom and Ket Kay would follow at his heels. But several of the bandits still carried their guns. The risk was too great.

"First we eat," said the Karen. "We have come a long way. The meat is soon ready, and the men are tired and hungry."

"Very well," agreed the leader. "But I do not like the

way that elephant is watching me. Take him away. Get him out of my sight."

The Karen and four torchbearers with guns led Haji and the elephant a short way into the jungle. Haji shook his head when they paused.

"No," he said. "The elephant is hungry, too. Find a place where he has something to eat."

They went on for several minutes until they found a more suitable place. As they paused again, Haji suddenly had an idea. Why not hobble the elephant rather than chain him to a tree? The bandits were not likely to know how fast a hobbled elephant could travel. Quickly he stooped and began chaining the front legs of the elephant loosely together.

"What are you doing?" cried the Karen. "We are not stupid. Chain him to a tree, a big tree."

Haji hesitated. Beads of perspiration broke out on his face as he stared down at the chain in his hand, one end of which was already secured to the elephant's front leg.

He had one hour—just one small hour—in which to make good his escape. Unless he made his move now time would run out on him.

He looked up at the grim faces about him. "Chaining him to a tree is no good," he said thickly. "He would finish all the grass and leaves within reach in a few minutes. It would only sharpen his appetite and make him angry."

"No more talk!" snarled the Karen. "Chain him to the tree and be quick."

Still Haji hesitated until the sharp prod of a rifle forced him to do as he had been told. His fingers trembled as he fastened the end of the chain in his hand around a large tree. His captors, watching his every move, held their torches close.

Then the Karen himself inspected the chain. At last he seemed satisfied that it was properly secured to the elephant's leg and to the tree.

As Haji was marched back to camp his legs wobbled under him. He felt weak, and his pulse beat wildly. But as he hunkered down near the cook fire, the racing within him slowly quieted. He could feel Ket Kay staring at him, but avoided looking at him.

The sambur deer was browning nicely and sputtering and giving off savory odors. Haji sniffed and licked his lips. Hunger became a pleasant pain in his stomach.

Minutes passed. The sambur deer was almost done now. Haji began listening for a sound in the jungle, a very special sound. He knew almost to the second when Majda Koom would finish eating the grass and leaves within reach of his trunk.

Then suddenly it came—the moment Haji had been waiting for. There was a sharp metallic snap. They all heard it. They also heard the clink, clink, clink of a dragging chain as Majda Koom hurried off into the darkness of the jungle.

Haji joined the others in a wild scramble for torches.

He caught hold of Ket Kay's arm. "Stay here," he whispered.

Then he ran with the others as they rushed into the darkness after their precious pack animal.

A few moments later he returned alone to join Ket Kay at the cook fire, chuckling to himself.

Ket Kay was frightened. "Haji, what happened? What are you going to do?"

"First, we will need some dinner," he answered, and he carved a generous slice of roasting meat for Ket Kay and for himself. Then he sat down to enjoy it.

The fading sounds of the chase made him laugh aloud, for he knew Majda Koom would leave them far behind in a matter of minutes. The will of the gods had been served.

"How stupid of those barbarians!" he said, laughing. "They did not know that an elephant has to be chained by his hind leg, and with a strong chain."

"What did you do?" asked Ket Kay, glancing nervously back over his shoulder.

"I had only the light hobble chain on his front leg and I tied the other end of that to the tree. I knew he could break it with one tug of his trunk. Majda Koom did the rest."

"But Majda Koom is running away," said Ket Kay. "What will happen to him? What can we do?"

Still chuckling, Haji carved another thick slice of meat for each of them. "Now it is time to go," he said.

143

And, chewing on the meat with relish, they started off into the darkness.

They had traveled for some time before Ket Kay spoke again. "Where do we go, Haji?"

"To meet Majda Koom," answered Haji. "He is a creature of habit. He will feast on bamboo in the hills during the night. Then he will head back for a breakfast of kaing grass in his favorite nullah where I always find him." He laughed again. "There is no hurry. We will reach the nullah long before Majda Koom has finished his breakfast."

The sun was well up the following morning when Haji rode proudly into the elephant camp on the head of Majda Koom. There were shouts and cries as people came running, Ket Kay among them, for he had arrived an hour earlier with news of their capture by the New Brotherhood.

"The tree chopper escaped!" cried Ket Kay. "But they caught Chan Tha, and he has confessed."

One of the small boys yelled, "The soldiers have gone into the hills to look for the outlaws."

Oo Yan pressed through the crowd, followed by Thakin Jensen and the red-faced inspector.

In almost a whisper, Oo Yan said, "What is more important is that you and Majda Koom have come back to us unharmed."

"Well done, Haji!" cried Thakin Jensen.

Haji ordered his elephant down. He stepped to the ground with all the dignity he could muster—to prove to the inspector that he could act like a mature person.

Turning to the thakin, Haji said, "By your leave, Thakin Jensen, I most report the loss of one hobble chain and one drag chain."

"Sorry to hear that," replied the thakin soberly. "As you know, the loss of any company property must be paid for by the oozie responsible. That means that I shall have to take the cost of the two chains out of your salary."

The red-faced inspector coughed politely. "Oh come now, Jensen, aren't you being a bit hard on the lad? After all, it isn't every day that an oozie is called upon to rescue his elephant from bandits, you know."

The two men glanced at each other, and suddenly they were laughing. "Seriously, Haji, we wouldn't think of asking you to pay for the chains," said the thakin, smiling. You risked your life to bring back the company's most valuable elephant, and that is something we can never repay you for."

"But, Thakin, I did not do it for the company," confessed Haji.

"Of course you didn't. You did it for the love of your elephant," said the thakin. He reached out and took Haji gently by the shoulders. "That is what makes you a great oozie, Haji. I wish we had more like you."

The inspector coughed politely. "So do I," he said.

His face did not seem so red anymore, and his blue eyes twinkled with humor. "I did not know that good oozies could come in such small sizes," he said.

Haji looked up at Thakin Jensen. "Does that mean—"

The thakin nodded. "Yes, Haji. To put it plainly, you are the oozie of Majda Koom from now on. We would want no other."

Ket Kay jumped up and down and cheered, and others joined in.

Haji had to blink his eyes to keep from being blinded by tears.

"I can see you are very tired," said the thakin. "Why don't you run along now, both of you, and get some sleep."

As Haji mounted his elephant, so happy he could hardly keep from crying, the inspector called out to him.

"The next time you find a large log in the sand I should like to watch when you dig it up. What you did with that last log is truly remarkable!"

Haji and Majda Koom had almost reached the edge of the jungle when Ket Kay cried out. "Thank you, Haji. Thank you for saving my life and—and for everything."

Haji smiled as the words echoed in his head. They had not gone far before he realized how very tired he was. "Take us some place where we can rest, big brother," he said softly.

Leaning forward he rested a cheek against the top of

his elephant's head, took a deep breath, and closed his
eyes. Where they were going was not important. All that
mattered now was that he had become a real oozie at last,
and that no one would ever, ever, ever take the mighty
Majda Koom, lord of all elephants, away from him again.

ABOUT THE AUTHOR

Willis Lindquist is a lawyer and freelance writer of articles, adult fiction, and children's books. He has traveled extensively, having circled the globe with a camera and typewriter doing travel articles for various newspapers and magazines. Mr. Lindquist presently lives in New York City.

ABOUT THE ARTIST

Don Miller has illustrated over thirty books, numerous magazine articles, and several film strips. A freelance photographer as well, Mr. Miller has traveled through eleven countries in Africa researching traditional and contemporary African art and artists. The photographs from there along with his oil paintings and graphics have been exhibited in numerous group and one-man shows. He lives in Montclair, New Jersey, with his wife and two sons.